About the Author

V. R. Wilson graduated first in History, and then in Philosophy and the History of Education. Later she gained a Master's Degree in Education Law and Administration. After a short but varied career, a caring role followed – parents then husband. Her hobby of travelling and membership of various public bodies allow her little time to be idle.

Dedication

To those whose lives have touched mine and whom I
think of fondly.

V. R. Wilson

THE SOURING OF SWEET CHARITY

REVIEW COPY
Not For Resale

AUSTIN MACAULEY
PUBLISHERS LTD.

A CIP catalogue record for this title is available from the British Library.

ISBN 9781786124470 (Paperback)
ISBN 9781786124487 (eBook)

www.austinmacauley.com

First Published (2017)
Austin Macauley Publishers Ltd.
25 Canada Square
Canary Wharf
London
E14 5LQ

Acknowledgments

In a letter in 1598 Francis Bacon wrote *'opportunity makes a thief'*

Chapter 1

"Cymran? Cymran? Where's that?" During her five weeks travelling, the name of the island which, for the last fifteen years, Gina Fiddes had called home had not been known to most of the people she had met during her trip. This had not been a great surprise. Before moving to Cymran to live, except for the name, she, too, had no other knowledge of this small island state.

In answer to 'where?' and 'how big?' Gina had told interested inquirers that Cymran was to be found off the coast of Zanlandia. At least, the name of the nearby mainland had resulted in some recognition but only because some recalled its national football team's brief moment of glory, a few years before, when it unexpectedly defeated two giants of the game in an international championship. Even so, Gina has doubted any knew exactly where on the map Zanlandia, and thereby Cymran, could be found.

Addressing the matter of size, Gina had stated that there were island countries smaller than Cymran which was 300 kms (180 miles) in length and a consistent 135 kms (81 miles) in width if she had recalled correctly. A range of mountains stretching across the island, the peaks of which varied in height from 1000-1500 metres (roughly 3-4000ft), divided it into two distinct halves. This natural separation had an important bearing on Cymran's history and development.

Over the centuries, the original population had been killed off, or absorbed through conquest, leaving only two versions of the native language, still spoken by a minority, as a reminder of their existence. Once mineral wealth had been discovered, which led to a century of heavy industry in the South, further newcomers had arrived and settled. By the present day, however, the diversity of the population's origins is reflected only in the vast variety of names and surnames. Unity of language had come when the island, like nearby

Zanlandia, had become a dependency of the British Crown, leading to the adoption of English as the 'lingua franca'. In fact, Cymran had been a more cohesive whole when a dependency than in the years following 1989 when independence had been granted.

Since self-rule, the gulf between North and South had become more marked. Through being the largest town on the island Fridcar had become the designated capital, a status the place had assumed long before. Once the Legislative assembly had been established there, the previously scattered administrative, government departments had been moved to the city. This action, and various other policies, had served only to highlight the divide and a not unjustified claim that the South benefitted much more than the North from the budget spend. In consequence, the call for the island to become a federation of two states had heightened. The discovery of oil off the northern coast had made this idea, or even total separation from the South, attractive propositions to many.

Ignoring the politics, the island with its temperate climate, its beautiful beaches, as well as stunning coastal and mountain scenery, was a pleasant place in which to live or to holiday. The main difficulty with respect to tourism was that it had no large airport to cater for long haul flights. In truth, Cymran had only one real airport, namely that at Fridcar from where a very good service of shuttle flights operated to Manlah, Zanlandia's main international airport. The North, however, had been neglected, with shuttle flights to Manlah in service for just twelve months.

This new service operated from the air defence base in Valeria situated on the northern coast. Gina had blessed its introduction because this new venture saved what otherwise would have been a long and tedious beginning and end to her trip. Previously, the alternatives would have been to travel by ferry across a stretch of water notorious for its currents and bumpiness, followed by a drive to Manlah International Airport, or instead driving the scenic but winding road down to Fridcar to take a flight from there to Manlah.

Not surprisingly, having been so positive in her thoughts about the benefits of flights to Valeria, Gina had been very disappointed to hear, on arriving at the relevant gate at Manlah, that there was going to be a delay. Not everybody amongst the waiting passengers had accepted the news quietly. Some had feared it might be an excuse to combine flights as a load of only thirty passengers was far below the plane's capacity. Their pessimism had been unfounded because after twenty minutes, the call to board had been given. Actually the delay had resulted in quite a bit of a chat amongst the group. Some of it had been very good-humoured whilst some had been quite negative and full of complaints.

Chapter 2

From the conversations the delay had stimulated, Gina had gathered that twenty of the passengers were about to holiday in Cymran, the majority making their first visit. Except for herself and another couple, the rest, and most complaining, had been business men. One of them, David Johannes, she did know by sight and to nod to, but no more. In consequence, it had surprised Gina that he had chosen to sit beside her despite the ample provision of seats.

Although the man could be charming, he was also generally recognised to be egotistical and opinionated. His successful career as a folk singer had taken him away from his father's law firm but it had given him the money to have many business interests. It was, however, his fanatical politics of separation from the South of Cymran which Gina could not tolerate. Even though his tone had mellowed in the last couple of years, her disdain had led her to resign from a small charitable body once he had been appointed a fellow trustee, only Greg, her late husband, had known the reason for her resignation. Her dear Greg had been taken from her long before his time, a sentiment shared still by friends and acquaintances often with accompanying tears as well.

"You are brave to have gone travelling on your own," David Johannes had remarked, voicing an opinion others had expressed. He had followed this with another comment which had irked Gina even more.

"You'll have to find yourself a new husband or partner... that shouldn't be difficult. You're a good looking, smart and intelligent woman. And, what are you? Mid-forties, so still a young woman."

Most of what he had said, Gina had disregarded, even the complimentary guess at her age which, in fact, was fifty-five. However, she had felt compelled to take issue with the description of 'being brave', which did crop up a lot. It was uttered usually by women who proclaimed they could never contemplate going to a dinner function, or holiday, on their own - 'heaven forbid'! While to Gina, it seemed very sad that so many women could not define themselves without a partner. So, she had given her practised response:

"The word to use is not 'brave' but 'pragmatic'. Life goes on and when widowed, or divorced, you have to decide to do most of what you want to do on your own or not at all. Too many in their grief, and fear of loneliness, rush into new alliances that bring no real happiness... but maybe I am being over cynical!"

"You're right to correct me. When I think about it, your attitude is not a surprise. Of course, that is based on what I have heard about you rather than personal acquaintance."

"Hopefully all you've heard has been good. Perhaps, you should not answer that!" she had said laughingly although continuing to wonder what he had heard, and from whom? After that the conversation had been mainly about Cymran and its beautiful scenery which had made the sixty-minute flight pass quickly.

Before hurrying to disembark, David Johannes had enquired again whether Gina was sure that she did not require a lift home, emphasising it would be no trouble to detour a few miles. She had to admit that, when not irritated as he had been about the delay, or ranting about his political viewpoint, the man did have some kind of charisma. According to rumour, he was a 'lady's man', hence why his two marriages failed.

When waiting for her luggage, Gina had received a text from her friends, and nearest neighbours, who had insisted on driving her to Valeria when departing to avoid long term parking costs at the airport. The text had said; 'c. u. later, Look 4 D.H. Love F+L'. To have been greeted by Fay and Lars would have been great but Gina had not been very cheered to learn the task of transporting her home had been delegated to D.H., namely Don Hale. Having been critical in her mind about one man already, she had felt guilty about having unfavourable thoughts about another so soon afterwards. It went against her usual tolerance of people, still her cheery smile on entering the arrivals concourse had disguised her inner annoyance.

There at the barrier, smiling broadly at his expression of humour in holding a notice bearing her name 'Mrs Gina Fiddes', had been Don Hale, her unexpected escort home. He had greeted Gina fondly which had been warming especially as he was a tall, quite distinguished looking man. When relaxed, he could be good company but, as far as Gina was concerned, his extreme aversion to spending any money condemned him. To his two daughters, their father's determination to guard every cent was to be applauded, even encouraged, because his miserly carefulness meant their inheritance was to be sizeable. In fact, they would rather certify their father if he should have any thoughts about marrying again. If they had been aware of his trip to the airport to collect her, then Gina could well imagine the concern this gesture would have caused them. Following up on his joke with the name card, Gina had passed her case over to him and said: "Right Jeeves, where's the car?" Then, once in it, and the engine had been started, she had fixed her gaze on the petrol gauge. Don prided himself on driving between two points with the minimum of petrol in the tank.

"For you," he had remarked, anticipating some observation, "I put in an extra couple of litres."

"Big deal," she had retorted sharply. "What will it cost me? Dinner on the way back?"

Immediately after uttering the question, she had known that she had fallen into a foreseen trap.

"That would be very nice," he had smiled. "After all, you don't want to be making a meal on arriving home."

Chapter 3

The day following her homecoming, Gina had risen early feeling quite refreshed and in good spirit. Although her last five weeks had been very busy, with several flights and changes in time zones, her stamina had held out well allowing her to enjoy every minute. She fervently hoped that jet lag and tiredness stayed at bay for she had guessed that she would not be given the opportunity to ease herself gently into things on returning home.

By eight thirty, the phone had rung twice, the callers welcoming her back. The third call soon after had come from Fay which had not been unexpected. All Gina had done, the previous evening, had been to text the couple that she had arrived home safely and that the invitation to dinner the following evening was accepted gratefully, with 'can't wait to see you both... G' added to the end. The kind invitation had been on the answering machine. However, she had known that Fay's curiosity about Don's readiness to act as chauffeur would not have been able to wait until the evening to be satisfied.

Apparently, Don had inquired several times as to when exactly Gina had been due to return. When he had asked again just days before her arrival, Fay had suggested the change of duties which, she had emphasised, he had been glad, even eager, to do.

"Thank you very much," Gina had retorted somewhat acidulously. "Now tell me what it cost you? It cost me a meal."

"Ouch," Fay had exclaimed, quite shocked. "What happened to you during your travels?"

"Apologies, apologies!" Her own sharpness had embarrassed Gina who had tried, without really succeeding, to explain. "You know that you, and other worshippers at St. Jude's treat Don as some charitable cause to be looked after, given meals and so on. The excuse you all use is that men don't cope well on their own when widowed, and he is only too happy to have you all fussing."

Before Fay could respond, Gina had hastened to give her Don's reason, hoping afterwards to change the subject. "He wanted to know if I would be going to the forthcoming Business Club Dinner, the speaker being of special interest to him. If yes, he would apply for a ticket, not having attended these dinners for a while, his hope was to have company."

"There I knew it," Fay had declared excitedly, "he does fancy you."

"You're on to a lost cause even St. Jude couldn't remedy. Gosh, sorry have to go. No doubt you can hear someone impatiently ringing the door bell, see you this evening."

Literally Gina had felt she had been saved by the bell, at least for a while. Fay's romantic dreams for her were well intended but, as a matchmaker, she did not listen and was on to a lost cause. More than once, she had told Fay that she and Don were incompatible. While his occasional company might be pleasant enough, it did come at a price besides leading to unwanted speculation and inevitably the wrath of his daughters.

The previous day, although she had guessed she knew the answer, she had felt compelled to ask Don why he had not sent off for two tickets when details of the dinner had been received? He should have known there would be no shortage of applications to attend. If she had not taken the other ticket from him, he could have invited one of his daughters to accompany him. This suggestion had been met with an irked response.

"You know why," he had snapped. "Neither would appreciate being second choice. Furthermore, both, like their respective spouses, are boring company."

"Do I hear a back-handed compliment?" Gina had inquired mischievously but Don had not been amused so she had hurried to ask him to update her on the news and occurrences in her absence.

Only when reflecting, whilst on her way to answer the door, had it registered that Don had not asked her anything about her holiday. Still, he had said it was good to see her back which could be interpreted favourably.

Chapter 4

The person impatiently ringing the door bell had been the postman, the box overflowing with Gina's mail being somewhat heavy. For this reason, he had offered, very kindly, to carry it into the kitchen for her, setting it down on the table with the remark: "It will take you quite a while to go through that lot." His prediction had been right, it had taken a solid three hours merely to sort out what was rubbish to be disposed of in a bin bag immediately; papers that she would need to read, but later, and the most important pile needing to be addressed quickly.

Her mail had reminded Gina how busy she was through her consultancy and facilitator work, along with her membership of a couple of public bodies. The latter did not pay, not even an honorarium, the island's government believing the prestige of being appointed reward enough! Yet, the commitment which membership required did seem to grow, but this had helped her through the initial acute pain of bereavement.

While away, however, Gina had reviewed her life and commitments quite seriously. In fact, she had returned almost fully convinced it was time to consider selling up and moving away from the island which, over fifteen years, had become dear to her. The move to Cymran to live had enabled Greg and herself to get over a very traumatic incident in their lives of which their new friends knew nothing. Neither had regretted their decision to stay silent on the subject which continued to occasion tears.

The timely arrival of her friend Petra had broken Gina's run of sad memories and although her visitor had noticed her watery eyes, she had not pried as to the reason. Instead, hoping that Gina had not eaten lunch, she had opened a hamper containing a picnic for them to enjoy while she heard all about Gina's fabulous trip. Always very theatrical, Petra had stressed that she wanted to experience, through Gina's account, every detail of the adventure she so envied.

Petra's husband Bob kept her dangling on promises 'one day' one of his projects would yield the wished for fortune. So far none had and a lot of money had been squandered. No one could work out why Petra had remained so loyal and protective. Her two sons had never appreciated the sacrifices she had made for them and had escaped to far corners of the world as soon as they could. Once, Petra had confided that her outward cheeriness and confidence was a mask, that beneath there was frustration but Bob had been her choice for a husband for better, or worse, and things were never that bad. This had made Gina believe that, deep in her heart, Petra was convinced that the promised 'one day' would come and Bob would strike gold! While waiting, she did wish Petra used her own talents.

Meanwhile, Gina had been happy to admit, Petra's visit had cheered her greatly. It had given her a chance, through her narrative, to appreciate how good the trip had been and what wonderful experiences it had provided. Her audience of one had lapped up every detail and had been so delighted with the collection of trinkets from the places Gina had visited. Thus, late afternoon when leaving, Petra, in warmly hugging Gina had declared:

"I've been on a magic carpet with you and the pictures I have in my mind are so vivid I could sit down and paint them."

"Then, please do so," Gina had implored. "You have a talent to draw and paint, please start using it for your own profit and to fulfil your own dreams."

Waving 'goodbye' as she drove off Petra had shouted "I promise," but Gina had not dwelt on the hope. In any case, she had not realised the time and she had a few things to which to attend before changing and walking over to the Nielsons' for dinner. One of her immediate tasks had been to phone Maxim Xavier in response to a letter and message requesting her to contact him immediately on getting home, and she felt guilty she had not responded earlier. The call had lasted about ten minutes and yet when it ended Gina had been no wiser regarding the urgency to meet. The very next day, in fact, at ten o'clock which at least had meant no long period of suspense and wondering.

Chapter 5

Her friends, Fay and Lars Nielson, had said half past six, and as Fay opened the door to greet Gina, the clock in the hallway had been striking the half hour. A car in the driveway had indicated she would not be the only guest and she had wondered who else had been invited. However, before taking her through to the lounge Fay had told her that to make it a party of six at the table, she had invited Grace and James Samuel as well as Don. Instantly on hearing the Samuels were there, Gina had known it would not to be the pleasant, relaxed evening she had expected. All that could be hoped for was that James Samuel's reputation as a colossal bore had been exaggerated.

The Samuels had lived in the locality for some five years but Gina had become acquainted with them only marginally through Fay and Lars, and even then mainly with Grace. Her husband, James, a civil engineer was proud to boast about the projects worked on all over the world and from which he had done well. Thus, during the evening, Gina's recent travels had provided him with lovely opportunities to regale everyone with his anecdotes. In any case, whatever the topic of conversation, he had to dominate, his being the definitive view on all subjects. His wide experience, travels and age, 'being three score years and ten', made him a veritable sage.

Grace Samuel's attempts to stop her husband being at what she called his 'loquacious best' had failed to silence him. Instead he had countered that Gina and Don were a new audience, unacquainted with his tales! This had made Gina very grateful that she had said, in advance, that she needed to be home no later than nine thirty. It had enabled her to make her escape just as James Samuel announced that he would summarise for them the global economic situation and steer them on to the world's best investment opportunities. Her necessary departure had been deemed a pity, but then hearing Don say that he would escort Gina home because, in any case, he had no money for investment, had not gone down well.

"Remember we're giving you a lift home, so don't dawdle," James had instructed sharply.

Once the two had left the property, Don's annoyance had exploded dramatically.

"That man is odious! Why were Samuels invited? Surely Fay and Lars don't count them as friends? And to impose them on us, that was unforgiveable."

"Now be fair, it was not that bad and I suppose Fay sympathises with Grace who is Captain of the Women's Golf Team of which she's a member. Moreover, I think that they would have thought we would cope better than most… so think of it as a compliment."

"That's one way of looking at it," he had replied without conviction before falling silent for quite a few minutes.

While Gina had expected Don to make some negative comment about golf which he considered overconsumed people's passions, as did a whole list of other activities, he had surprised her by revealing some quite unexpected information.

"Let me tell you something about the Samuels, but keep it to yourself."

It was unlike Don to gossip, or to pass comment except when he was sure of his facts, so Gina had been agog to know what secret he intended to confide.

"I doubt if anyone hereabouts, not even Fay and Lars, know that they have a daughter. Actually, I would state nobody in this area is aware of this."

Gina had been informed the couple had a son who, from a very early age, had lived in a home because of his autism. No one had ever mentioned anything about a daughter. On the contrary, she had heard Grace say that the mental condition of her only child, a son, had distressed her. So Gina had wondered how Don knew differently and had become eager to learn more from him.

Don had begun by stating that Grace was not the actual mother which meant that what Gina had heard her say was true. This daughter Don had revealed, allegedly was James' child born from another relationship whom they had officially adopted when the child was four, a decision which the couple had lived to regret. On becoming a teenager this girl had become a handful and made Grace's life a misery during James' absences. Only money and influence had bailed her out of serious trouble. Such had been the situation, Neri had been sent to a school for wayward children in America after which she had gone to college there. Thereafter, nothing had been heard of her, or her whereabouts, for years. Then, much to the dismay of the Samuels, she had returned to Cymran some seven years back, married and with two children. It was her reappearance which had prompted the couple to move north.

Those who had known Neri from a child continued to doubt she had changed her ways. It had surprised them how quickly and easily she had been appointed to a position of responsibility. However, none had been shocked to gather she had left that post under something of a cloud. Yet, in spite of this blot on her C.V., she had landed a similar job almost immediately afterwards with promotion following quickly. Money and influence had been the general supposition for her 'lucky' breaks!

On hearing all this, there had been many questions Gina had wanted to ask being, therefore, very disappointed to be told by Don that he did not want to be drawn further on the subject than the summary he had given.

"Allow me just one small query," she had begged, "the name Neri is so unusual, is it a shortened name?"

"Short for Nerissa, I believe," Don had replied adding a query of his own, "Does it mean something to you. I sensed when I said 'Nerissa' that it did."

Unfortunately, she had a feeling of uncomfortable familiarity, not with the name, but with what she had heard. If she was right in this, then she had to agree totally with the description, "devious and an inveterate liar' which Don had quoted.

"No," she had answered feeling disconcerted. "Thanks for trusting me with the information, and for escorting me home. Better hurry back. Remember your orders."

Grimacing at the prospect of another hour listening to James Samuel, Don had not appreciated her reminder though he had managed a cheery "see you" before departing.

Chapter 6

In case of unforeseen hold-ups and never wanting to arrive anywhere late, Gina had allowed herself more time than the estimated hour to get to 'Villa Cecilia,' the residence of Maxim Xavier. The urgent request for a meeting had continued to puzzle but during her journey she had given up trying to guess, accepting that she had no clue. Of one thing however, she had been sure, that there had to be a good reason for both the meeting and the haste.

At breakfast that morning, her thoughts had lingered over something else, namely what Don had disclosed while walking her home. An unexplained, but very strong, feeling had convinced Gina that James Samuel's 'daughter' was known to her. Yet, she had neither known a Neri, nor a Nerissa, nor even heard of those names before, of that she had been certain. Unhappily though, she had come across a Rissa who had claimed her name to be an abbreviation for Clarissa but then the truth had not been the said person's forte. It had been the character details which Don had given, too close for coincidence, which had nagged Gina into believing Neri, or Nerissa, or Rissa were all one and the same. If she was right, then it grieved and saddened her that others had not acknowledged their concerns about this woman, especially her untrustworthiness.

At least, once Gina started on her journey, she had put all her troubling thoughts aside. The road wound through pleasant countryside but it could lead to frustration when caught behind a lorry carrying a load of heavy logs and opportunities to overtake were very few. This problem luckily had not occurred but one major road works, not far from her destination, had made her grateful for the minutes of leeway she had allowed.

Arriving at the gates of 'Villa Cecilia', she had pressed the intercom to gain entry. The house within walled grounds, always looked to Gina like a plantation house in America's Deep South even though it was built of stone and not clapboard. It was modest in size, as were the grounds, considering it was owned by a multi-millionaire, but then Maxim Xavier was a quiet, modest man who kept a low profile. Thus, only a few knew that he was the generous benefactor of many a worthy cause.

Whenever she visited the Villa, Gina parked at the spot to which she had been directed on her first visit. This was by the Garage/Workshop block and near a small, well-appointed house occupied by Jane and Nico Gerrard. It had been the latter who had given her the parking instruction. Afterwards, with a broad smile, he had introduced himself by name, adding mischievously that he was 'Mr Xavier's Outside Boss'. Another of Nico's instructions had been to leave the keys in the vehicle so that maybe she would be surprised when leaving which she had been, the car had been washed and valeted. On each occasion afterwards, the same had happened and would again on this visit, she had hoped.

Chapter 7

Since that first encounter which went back ten years, Gina had become quite well acquainted with Jane and Nico namely through their fund raising activity for a Charity which she had worked hard to establish. While they may have guessed, she doubted if the two had been told of the invaluable initial help given by their boss. It was a secret shared by one other, besides herself, and the benefactor of course.

Once out of the car and approaching the main house, Jane had come hurrying towards Gina to greet her most cordially. Nico had appeared from behind her, his greeting just as warm. Both had expressed their hope she would have time for them before leaving. Standing at the door observing had been the man who had summoned her, Maxim Xavier. Not a man who would stand out in a crowd, ordinary might be the initial first impression of many as it had been hers but this seemingly quiet, unassuming, even nondescript individual 'just hid his light'. Being neither noticed, nor remembered from a crowd of people could have its advantages if the aim was to watch and listen. There were those who had got to power by possessing such attributes!

Fortunately, before Gina's thoughts had wandered further, Maxim's welcome had returned her to the present.

"Lovely to see you. It's been a while. Thanks for coming at such short notice and before you got back into stride after your trip, which I assume you thoroughly enjoyed."

Following Gina's assurance that the trip had gone smoothly and had been much enjoyed, Maxim had informed her that he guessed she must be very curious about his call but all would soon be revealed. Gina had a feeling, as they made their way to the rear terrace that he was quietly relishing the suspense he was creating.

While enjoying their coffee accompanied by Jane's delicious home cooked biscuits, they had caught up with each other's activities since their last meeting. Maxim had been keen to know if Gina felt as good as she looked. Acknowledging his genuine concern, she had mentioned that she had returned, almost a hundred percent, convinced that she should sell up and leave the island. To go where, to do what were issues she still had to resolve.

Maxim had appreciated the many reasons for her unsettled feelings but he had urged her not to rush into any decision:

"There are people who really care for you," he had stressed. "Never be too proud to talk, or ask for help, for yourself, I mean. I am aware of how good you are at asking for others, or for *causes*." The emphasis on the word 'causes' had made them both laugh.

At that opportune moment, Jane had arrived to tell them that 'the others' had been shown into the Library which moments later Gina and Maxim had entered. In the room, they had found two men in serious conversation about one of the rare books the Library contained. The older of the two men she had met before, he was Simon Bell, Maxim's solicitor. The tall, younger man in his late twenties had introduced himself stating he was Pascal Niven, an investigator in the employ of Mr Xavier.

"How very interesting," Gina had commented before turning to look directly at Maxim, "I can't wait to learn what this gathering is all about. Like Alice said in her 'Adventures in Wonderland', it is all getting 'curiouser and curiouser'."

Her observation had prompted no response other than smiles. However, all four had taken their place at the table which Gina had interpreted as a shared interest in starting discussion about whatever they had been called together to address. Thus it had annoyed her, that, when all seemed set to start, Pascal had found it necessary to go and fetch something, a departure that seemed totally unnecessary when all he had come back with was a red pen.

As he hastened to resume his place, he had repeated his apologies adding: "I assure you, Mrs Fiddes, that I am usually very well organised." Looking directly at him to acknowledge his apology, Gina felt that there was something inexplicably different about him. Deciding to gamble she had inquired: "Is this a test? Something tells me I shook hands not with you but your double... oh, I get it... identical twins... and you've changed places." Without hesitation the response had been that she was mistaken. Not deterred, Gina had pronounced that she was definitely right, though inwardly she had felt some butterflies on hearing her confident declaration.

"Game over! Pierre go and bring your brother back." Then, following this instruction, Maxim had turned to Simon Bell.

"I told you Gina would not be long in seeing through our attempted deception. She seems to have a sixth

34

sense, intuition, or whatever, which tells her when things are not as they should be. Alas, it has not been possible for her always to prove immediately what she suspects."

"Thank you for that testimonial," Gina had responded as the twins Pascal and Pierre Niven returned to the Library. When they stood side by side, the slight difference in height and weight could be seen on close scrutiny.

Then, when they had taken their seats on opposite sides of the table, Maxim had revealed that having identical twins as investigators had advantages which he did not detail. Instead he announced that it was time to make known that they had been gathered together to talk about a Charity, namely its Board of Trustees and its main officers. Gina had known at once which one was meant and had felt at a loss as to why Maxim had not forewarned her that this was to be the topic?

Chapter 8

Why all the mystery? What was to be unfolded? Why were the others present? Gina's mind had abounded with questions. She had recognized also that the topic would open up some very sensitive as well as bitter and hurtful issues for her. Things which should not have happened if the overall regulation had been effective. The weakness which all too often damages laudable causes is poor governance. This can occur when Chief Officers dominate the Chair person, or vice versa, or when both are in cahoots. The resulting scenario from any of the above is the same, namely that Trustees are expected to rubber stamp everything without question. This many are happy to do while those who object get tired of fighting losing battles and leave.

Poor governance by Trustees allows too many opportunities for abuses, a fact acknowledged but not yet remedied. Knowing all this and her enduring sensitivity on the subject, Gina had concluded that there had to be a very good and pressing reason for Maxim to open her wound and without prior warning. Even so, she was not sure she wanted to be reminded of what she regarded as an 'unjustified failure'.

Noticing her silence, Simon had commented that she was thinking hard and that he would guess it was about governance, or the lack thereof, and the consequences.

However, before she could respond, Maxim had interrupted to state that the meeting, though informal, would follow a specific order. He had then confirmed that they were indeed going to talk about the island's Angelus Charity.

"All of you know so well that each cent given in donations to a charity matters greatly and should not be squandered or misused. People work too hard for their money for their generosity not to be respected. This is why governance, already mentioned, is so important. Trustees are expected to give due diligence to their role as watchdogs."

Gina had never before experienced Marcus express himself with such passion. It seemed as if he had been addressing his feelings to others, not just the four of them and merely as an introduction.

"All Gina's pleadings for due diligence failed. Finally, when faced with blatant lies about her, very bruised and disheartened she resigned. This fabricated onslaught hitting her less than a month following her husband's sudden death. Still we shall start at the very beginning."

In inviting Gina to tell them all about the Charity from its start until she resigned, he had instructed her to treat them as people who had no knowledge at all of this organisation. Not having expected such a task, Gina had needed a couple of minutes to gather her thoughts consoling herself that the challenge was a far easier one than she had faced when asked to set up an emergency sky medical service by means of charitable donations. Just why she had been chosen to champion this cause had seemed a good place to start, prefaced by some comments about herself.

Chapter 9

Gina had thought it correct to presume that the Niven twins knew little about her except her name and so she had started her summary with the reason she and Greg had come to Cymran, as it was of relevance.

"Greg and I came to live on the island fifteen years ago wanting to make a new start after a traumatic and tragic incident in our lives. Cymran was chosen because we were bequeathed a small property not far from Fridcar."

Casting her mind back had brought a lump to her throat but she had pressed on stating that, only when they had moved to her present property, a year later, had their lives begun to fall into place again.

It had been at this time, based on her qualifications and experience, that she had been appointed to a newly established Emergency Services Trust Board, as one of the five Non-Executive Directors. This Board had been set up to improve the island's poor coverage by an ambulance service. At the time, there had been large municipalities, with up to 12,000 inhabitants which did not have access to any such emergency vehicles, nor any nearby. Yet the island could boast it had five world class hospitals, each with its own specialism.

From the time of Independence, the New Health Ministry had set out to encourage 'health tourism' by those who had the money to pay. It had known that the island's medical service was already superior to that of the nearby mainland state of Zanlandia and its neighbours. To further enhance this lead, the Republic's new government had spent a significant portion of the budget on establishing world class medical teams to attract patients from even further afield. Their payments were used to subsidise the State's Health Insurance Scheme paid into by all the inhabitants, thereby keeping the cost reasonable while offering residents an excellent service as well.

While this health policy had much to commend it, its budget share left no money for a patient transport system to get people into Hospital. If an area happened to have an ambulance, it was there either through the goodwill of the Department of Emergency and Security in that locality, or because a local benefactor had purchased the vehicle. In both circumstances, the Ambulance then depended on volunteers from the Civil Protection Group in that district to operate its vehicle. The new Board had a mammoth job to do, especially on the limited budget it had been given.

"Being new to the island, and fortunately not having had the need to be rushed into Hospital, I had no idea of the situation and its implications. Actually, all the Board Members of EST found themselves on a steep learning curve, and fast."

After stating that the first year had been hard but very positive in what had been achieved, Gina had claimed that there had been a downside to this. Very suddenly, the people had become more impatient and demanding, with even small villages wanting their own ambulance. When common sense prevailed and they had realised that their demands were utopian, the media had planted an alternative idea on which they could lobby… an emergency air service would make it possible for urgent cases to get their medical intervention as quickly as possible.

"Gina, was this the time the series 'M*A*S*H' was shown on the island's new T.V. channel?" Pierre had inquired with his brother Pascal adding a supplementary question;

"Was the Korean War the first time helicopters were used to transport patients? Being strapped on a stretcher outside the aircraft would be enough to kill many." Pascal's observation showing that he would not fancy the idea.

Noticeably irritated by this interruption, Simon Bell had told the Nivens to ask Gina for a history at some other time and that it was important to focus so the thread was not lost. Quietly, Gina assured the twins she would deal with their questions later and then she had continued.

"When the Government became aware of the call for an emergency air service following a T.V. programme on the subject, it had told the Board of EST, very emphatically, that its task, and priority, was establishing a fleet of land vehicles, and there was money only for this, not for helicopters. This clear dictum had placed the Board in an invidious position as the lobbyists, urged on by the media, believed it could set up the air service if it chose to and that it would be Government sponsored!

A point which Gina had considered important to stress had been the fact that it was only in the late 1990s, or in the early years of the twenty-first century that an air medical service had been established across the U.K.

Moreover, except in Scotland, these services depended on the sponsorship of Charities set up for the purpose. Cymran, therefore, had not been far behind when its Angelus Charity, and its initial one helicopter, became operational in 2005 with Aswanes in the South as its base. Thirty months later, a second helicopter had gone into service, its base Colemar in the North.

"Now, of course, I have to tell you just how the Angelus came to be established with its success masking a cancer within, the cells of which were there from the beginning. Not something I am proud of admitting."

Chapter 10

The lobbying for an emergency air medical service had not been well received by the Chairman of EST nor by Gina's fellow Non-executives who viewed air ambulances as a luxury when more land ambulances were needed. In any case, the Board had been given its orders which her colleagues had considered ended the matter. Thus it had greatly surprised Gina to be approached by the Chairman with a pressing request that she look into the possibility of setting up a Charity to fund an emergency air service. The factor which had persuaded her to accept the challenge, had been the total negativity of the other Non-executives. When they heard that she had accepted the challenge, they had considered her very foolish to take on such a project which they had described as a 'poisoned chalice'. All Gina had said in response had been that someone had to try, and if she was doomed to fail so be it.

Gina had attached one condition to her acceptance namely that two of the Directors of EST, namely the Directors of Operations and of Finance should be tasked to help her. Both had agreed in the knowledge, that their help and support would have to be in an 'unofficial capacity'. Without this agreement, Gina fully acknowledged she could not have picked up the gauntlet.

"Where? How? Do you start such a project, especially with no money granted for a feasibility study? What a daunting challenge you accepted! Doubt you would be so foolhardy again," Again it had been Pierre who had spoken and in replying Gina had agreed that she had been rash.

"Greg was so right to warn me that I would receive no thanks for my efforts. Then, he was so right with regard to many things."

After a pause, she had addressed the question of Where? And How? Or, at least, she had tried to, admitting that she had not appreciated what a stumbling block the 'chicken and egg' situation could be. She had explained that what she had been trying to say had been many wanted the 'chicken and egg' before they would consider giving any support. Later, when a service had been launched and had been operating successfully for a while, attitudes had changed with known names then becoming happy to be linked with the cause.

"Do you know that letters sent out to leading companies on the island inviting them to consider some measure of sponsorship for the idea yielded not a single offer? Letters to other organisations were similarly fruitless. Only fourteen out of the hundred people invited attended the first meeting to discuss the proposal. By the third meeting that number had gone down to three. I just could not believe it."

While the twins had agreed that going down to three would have been very disappointing, to be still turning up the three must have been very supportive to the idea. Their expression had shown that the latter part of their statement posed a question to which Gina had hurried to respond.

"Supporting an idea is one thing, working hard for it to become a reality is another. I wrote at length in my diary at the time of my great unease and that the thought of them, through default, becoming Trustees troubled me."

Immediately, Simon had asked why she had been of the opinion the three were not 'the right sort of people'. Intuition would have had to be her only answer at the time. All three were men of 'standing', known to each other and to the Director of Operations who had vouched for them. From the start, however, Gina had summed them up, quite correctly as 'passengers' who had neither the enthusiasm nor intention of actively participating in the task of drumming up support and money, that was for others to do. Their real interest lay only in the prestige, or kudos, that would be theirs when a Charity was established and an air emergency service successfully operated. There had been no way in the scheme of things at the time to prevent them becoming Trustees or sadly of preventing them believing the appointment was for life!

Quite plaintively, Gina had told her listeners that she had tried to step away but the Chairman of EST had pressed on her that it was incumbent on her 'to hang in there and carry on'. He had stressed that there were expectations by this time but he had been without helpful suggestions on the matter of money. The lack of funds she had thought would buy her some time, during which she would ensure that Trustees for the Charity, soon to be founded, could be appointed through a proper process. Circumstances, however, overtook her when she was told that Global Helicopters Ltd had a suitable helicopter available to lease from April 1, 2005, and that acceptance of this lease was expected.

The availability of this helicopter and five donations of £10,000 (Cymran's currency being based on Sterling) from five Doctors for the specific purpose of training paramedics for the Sky Medical Service, meant that the die had been cast. For Gina it had meant that the option of failing had been taken away, the necessary money had to be conjured up from somewhere. "And this is where Maxim stepped in to be my Saviour." His generosity still moved her, and she was quite unashamed of her tears.

Chapter 11

Gina admitted that, although she had pondered long and hard over the letter she had written to Maxim Xavier once she had posted it, her approach had worried her. She had asked very simply if she could meet with him to discuss a project, the value of which from his own personal experience, she believed, he would appreciate.

"Intriguing, but also rather vague" had been the verdict of the twins with which she had agreed but before she had time to explain why, Maxim had interrupted to say he would take up to next bit of the story. This had been a relief to Gina who had been unsure what Maxim might, or might not, want disclosed.

"I never ignore letters even though I get a surprising number of cheeky, and unwanted, begging ones," a statement uttered with a wry smile.

"With regard to that which I received from Gina, it was her name that drew my attention to it. Someone had mentioned the name to me, quite by chance and in a different context but very favourably, which persuaded me to agree to a meeting. After doing so, I did some further checking and discovered that both of us had experienced traumatic tragedies. Hers and Greg's being even greater than my own."

At this point, Maxim and Gina had exchanged glances, very similar to those shared at their first meeting, expressing empathy with each other. When he continued Gina had noticed that Maxim's tone had changed and his words were being spoken more slowly, more deliberately.

"Great anguish is not forgotten even if time dulls the heartache and memory tempers the desolation felt. When visiting the U.S. in 1997 my wife, son and sister-in-law were involved in a multiple pile up. All three were airlifted to Hospital but sadly, within hours, they died of their injuries. Still, through being transported by air to the region's best trauma centre, they were given that remotest, possible chance of surviving, but sadly as I have mentioned it was not to be. By coincidence, Gina knew of the tragedy, hence her approach."

As if to prevent any kind of comment, Maxim had hurried to urge Gina to take up the narrative once again, which she had done by explaining that her letter had been deliberately vague, not wanting her appeal to appear as emotional blackmail. She and Greg had been driving from the U.S. Airport towards which Maxim's family had been travelling at the time the accident occurred. Also it had been shown and reported on in the media and the name had been easy to remember. In addition, she and Greg had wondered how people coped with such personal, tragic events never thinking that, two years later, they would know at first-hand how it felt. A dramatic and horrendous incident had changed their lives as well.

Taking a very deep breath, her discomfort quite obvious even before she had uttered a further word;

"A wedding... it all happened at a wedding. Bride, groom, four bridesmaids, best man, two page boys and a hundred happy guests. Gillian, my twelve-year-old daughter had been so delighted to be one of those bridesmaids, the bride being distantly related. So not only were Greg and I there but my parents and maternal grandmother."

A pause had followed. Gina had needed to take another deep breath to keep hold of her emotions. Just noticing Simon's jerk of surprise when she had mentioned Gillian had so made her want to cry.

"There as well were Greg's parents, his brother and wife and son. The groom's father had worked alongside Greg's father for many years, resulting in a strong family friendship. On the eve of the wedding, we had enjoyed such a happy get together never imaging that it would be 'The Last Supper', very literally, for all except Greg and myself."

A flash of that happy scene on the eve of the wedding had caused Gina to stop briefly. She could hear her heart pounding from knowing what her continued account would have to relate. Conscious that the attention of those present had been concentrated upon her, she had resumed but more slowly and falteringly.

"The small historic Church was full and guests had to squeeze up in the pews which had added a special intimacy to the atmosphere... Everyone was so friendly, excited... eagerly anticipating."

While speaking, the voice of her grandmother had echoed clearly in her mind. Sitting beside Gina, she had told her that she would have to change her outfit before the Reception because it was identical to that of the groom's sister. It had delighted her grandmother to reiterate her preference anyway for an alternative outfit Gina had brought with her, being undecided. So, to make gran happy, and save any embarrassment she had whispered her agreement. Thus, before making their way to the Reception held in a marquee in the grounds of a Hotel, a little distance away from the Church, she and Greg had driven back to the Hotel at which they had been staying in order for her to change. At the time, it had seemed no big deal.

Although she had been trying hard to distance herself from the words she had been uttering, in her mind's eye Gina had been seeing, hearing, even smelling what happened next more vividly than for some time. In consequence she had speeded up hoping to make the task of continuing easier by doing so.

"When starting back, we heard an almighty explosive bang. The ground shook. Soon we were embroiled in traffic congestion which made us abandon the car. Hearing mutterings of a horrendous catastrophe, we quickened our pace to a frantic run, made harder by people and vehicles as we neared our destination. Then we froze in sheer disbelief at the scene from hell which confronted us."

The memory of that dreadful moment and the ghastly realisation of what it had meant had made Gina seem for a moment visibly dazed. Then, despite the tears which had been streaming down her face, Gina had stressed the next words hoping by doing so her listeners would try hard to imagine that dreadful scene and its tragic, as well as personal emotional implications.

"Absolute devastation! My God, you have no idea! Greg and I had family no more and now I don't even have Greg."

At this point, Gina's sad memories had overwhelmed her and, indicating with hand gestures that she wanted no one to follow her, she had rushed from the Library. Once outside her inner turmoil had subsided and anger at allowing her emotions to surface had taken over. After their initial despair and strong feeling of guilt at being alive, Gina and Greg believed they had recovered well. Both had appreciated that self-pity destroys, and life, however cruel and hard, had to be lived and remained precious. Thus, their stoicism, determination and love for each other had enabled them to pick up the pieces and make a new life for themselves on the island of Cymran.

Chapter 12

While Gina had been out of the room, Maxim had informed the others what tragic catastrophe had faced the couple on that fateful wedding day. A large hydrogen gas-filled dirigible, or air ship had exploded and crashed on the Marquee incinerating everyone within the venue and its vicinity. Though smaller, it had resembled the Hindenburg, or the R101, both of which had also crashed many, many years before. This airship had been on a demonstration flight from a nearby airfield, its owners and sponsors having been keen to show that such zeppelins were safe! They had been used by the Germans during World War One for bombing raids. In fact, they had operated quite safely for many years. Just what happened in this instance remained undetermined.

Hearing all this had led Pierre to declare with some passion: "More than ever now, I want that deceitful, woman and her 'three stooges' to be severely punished. They deserve long sentences if only for what they did to Gina, and so immediately after her husband's death. Even if they had known of her previous tragedy it would not have stopped them, they really are despicable people."

These words which Gina had overheard in approaching the Library and opening the door had heartened her. Suddenly, she had felt encouraged that something important had been uncovered which she desperately hoped would lead to positive changes, Maxim's generosity deserved that. So, after apologizing for her exit and presuming Maxim had told them what had caused the disaster, Gina had begun again with a question: "Did Maxim tell you about his generosity, without which the Angelus Charity could not have been set up? And this modest man wanted no acclaim! The source of the money to start operating was to be known only to myself and the Chairman of EST."

Maxim had mentioned he made a donation but not the amount. His promise of £1.5 million had caused Gina to leave that first meeting with him in stunned disbelief, pinching herself to ensure that she had not been dreaming. Despite her euphoria over his generosity, she had insisted that it could not be accepted unconditionally. She had stipulated that only £500,000 of the sum should be a gift while the rest should be considered as a loan to be repaid at the end of ten years, if not before should the governance of the Charity be considered unsatisfactory. At the time, Gina's main reason for insisting on such an agreement had been to show good faith, although as well her unease may have prompted her into such a clause. A similar concern may have influenced the Chairman of EST who unbeknown to Gina, had extended the clause to say that if Gina left the Charity due to reasons of dissatisfaction then the loan had to be repaid without delay. With the benefit of hindsight, it seemed uncanny that two people had believed such a safeguard to be wise and necessary. Suddenly, Gina had begun to wonder if the hastily summoned meeting concerned due process to request repayment of the million. The Charity was nearing its tenth anniversary and it was almost two years since she had ceased to be a Trustee. If she was truthful, Gina had never contemplated the money ever being recalled although there had been grounds to do so for a long time. The Board of Trustees as a corporate body had not given due regard to governance. If proof was wanted her continuing narrative would give it in abundance and throughout she had documented her concerns.

Chapter 13

Only Trevor Mason, the Chairman of EST, had congratulated Gina on getting the start-up funds for the Charity, claiming that he had never doubted that she would. The trio, as she had begun to call them, while greatly pleased had preferred to attribute the money to the efforts of Trevor Mason, but that for political reasons this could not be openly declared! Not unexpectedly, Gina had felt somewhat slighted that her now fellow Trustees could not recognise her hard work, yet it had not been a total surprise. In all honesty, neither had been the fact that she had not been chosen as chairperson of the new charity, a position Trevor had advised her to assume and announce on the day the Angelus was launched.

What had come as a surprise had been the Trio's appointment of the Director of Operations of EST as the Chairman and even more so his acceptance. This action deliberately went against what had been stipulated very clearly at the outset, namely that the two Directors of EST, (operations and finance) could only act as advisers. Their 'unofficial' involvement had been allowed only in order to get Gina to accept the challenge. The deliberate contravention of this tacit agreement had spelt out to her a calculated plan.

Even when the Director of Operations received instructions to resign as Chairman which, of course, had been expected, it had been Marcus Temple who had stepped into the position of Chairman, through being already the appointed Deputy. This completed part one of the plan while the choice of Felix Morgen as the new Deputy, or Vice Chair achieved the second part.

Greatly stressed had been the practical reasons for their 'selection' namely that both lived near Aswanes from where the helicopter was to operate and where, as a result, the Charity's office would be established. The two would be near at hand to keep a watching brief, or provide any direction required! Had it been down to Gina, or to the Chairman of EST, the helicopter would have operated from the small airport near the central town of Tralyn. For various reasons, however, Global Helicopters Ltd, from which the helicopter was leased, thought differently and insisted the small airfield near Aswanes should be the base.

For the Trio, this insistence had been excellent news and very quickly they had put forward a strong supporting argument for a southern base: the South had more large conurbations, more businesses and organisations and, therefore, more people from whom to seek financial support. All this was true and had easily overshadowed Gina's counter argument that if the helicopter was based at Tralyn it could serve both North and South quite widely, until sufficient funding allowed the Charity to lease a helicopter for the North. In addition, had it been a decision for which she was solely responsible, April 1, 2005, would not have been the date on which the Sky Medical Service became operational. This was because it had allowed only eight weeks to get organised and to get staff appointed. Suddenly, there was pressure to rush to which the Trio had been happy to succumb.

Chapter 14

The rush to become operational greatly suited the machinations of the Trio who had wasted no time in assuming control. Without prior consultation, or any discussion of the job description for the post of General Manager, Gina had discovered that an appointment had been made during her short period away from the island, her absence providing an excuse as to why she had not been informed of what had taken place. Unhappily, this set a precedent for which some pressing reason had been always available to conveniently offer in explanation.

The young man appointed to be the first General Manager proved to be a pleasant surprise to Gina and, during his time with the Charity, she had never had any cause to be disappointed, nor critical of his work and commitment. However, Tony Rohm on first meeting her had quietly confided that he had not been the first choice. The person who had initially been offered the post had turned it down a day or so later. This had been a great disappointment to Marcus who had sought the person's application. In view of this, Tony had accepted that he would have to work exceptionally hard to prove himself to the Trio but Gina had been right in fearing that any praise would not be forthcoming. Despite his untiring efforts to raise funds, he never received a supportive word from them, after all he was merely doing his job! Their attitude had grieved Gina because she knew how hard it was to raise money for a cause which had yet to prove itself.

At the start Tony had only one full time and one part time staff member to help him with his fund- raising activity, which had to be concentrated in the South, a situation about which Gina had no complaint. One young man however enthusiastic and hardworking could not cover the whole of the island. Consequently, to achieve her aim of raising sufficient funds as quickly as possible for the North to have a service, Gina herself had taken on the task of gaining support for this in Cymran's northern sector. This had not been easy when only the South had a helicopter and a sky med service. People had feared that their money would be used merely to support the South and their disapproval had been hard to overcome. More than once, Greg had posed the question whether the Trio were as hard working?

In view of Gina's reluctance to answer his query, he had assumed quite correctly that the answer was no and he gained confirmation of this when Tony made a rare sortie North to visit Gina. Without prompting, Tony had let it be known that neither Marcus nor Felix participated in any fund-raising but that following a challenge issued to him by Gina, Damon Long the third member of the Trio, had got him a sponsored vehicle, the running costs of which his father had agreed to pay. Out of Gina's hearing, Tony had told Greg that Damon was a short cocky individual, full of his own importance who liked to be noticed. This was why he had volunteered to do all media interviews with regard to the Charity. Tony, like Gina, had no quarrel with this for it meant that Damon was doing something and usually doing it well.

"When he began working for the Charity, on finding himself with only 'one and a half' staff members, Tony had imposed on staff working for his father to help him out with the paperwork. After nine months, two further full time staff were appointed and they all became a very good team. What is more, they were very good at keeping me informed of everything which was going on. The responsibility for the slippage with regard to Trustee Board meetings lay with Marcus. This was as much a source of annoyance to Tony, and his team, as it was to me. Oh! It was so hard being two hundred miles away."

The anguish which this had caused Gina was still reflected in her voice especially as she had never succeeded in getting Marcus, as Chairman, to concede that Trustees needed regular meetings to fulfil their role and responsibilities.

Being such a sore and regretted issue, it had cheered Gina greatly to hear Simon Bell acknowledging her frustration, and sympathising with it. "Believe me, it is appreciated how hard you tried. We are learning a lot which is all very significant. So do carry on." While everything had been happening over the years, she had never detailed the whole scenario as she had been attempting to do for Maxim, Simon and the twins and, as never before, she had amazed herself by her perseverance. With more to tell that was not good, she had begun to feel uneasy about what to others might seem foolish, pointless stubbornness on her part.

In hindsight, Gina had to recognize that such a verdict would be justified, but that was with hindsight. At the time, there had been the positive to keep her going. The new service was doing good work; it was saving lives. Additionally, if truthful, she would have to admit that there had been some satisfaction from being a constant thorn in the side of the Trio. Giving them free rein by resigning had been something Gina had determined against because she had feared the consequences for the Charity, especially financially.

Chapter 15

If the Board of Trustees of Cymran's Angelus Charity had been subjected to close scrutiny and assessment, it would have been criticised, very justifiably, for falling below standard. Gina had no qualms in making such an assertion. Yet, in spite of this, so much that was positive, and lasting had been realised, and was continuing to be achieved through the efforts of others, certainly not the Trio. In the North as well as the South, a lot of friends had been found who worked quietly and hard to raise the necessary funds. People, in their sadness and grief, made donations in memory of their loved ones in recognition of the helicopter's front line work.

Each mission undertaken had led to increasing awareness of what was being accomplished, with sadness increasing when incidents happened in areas not covered, and where speedy intervention might have saved a life. Such a situation in the North, when it had been believed that the life of a young woman involved in a nasty car accident might have been saved if she been airlifted to Hospital, motivated her parents to become active fund-raisers. In the space of two years, they had urged and cajoled the people of six coastal villages near where they lived to raise £150,000 for the Charity. This money, however, they had refused to hand over until they had been assured the North would get a Sky Med service and a person from their community, following a local vote, became a Trustee.

The work of this group had illustrated to Gina the growth of support for the service throughout the Northern area. This kind of effort and the sum raised could not be ignored by the Board, nor could the stipulation that the North wanted a Sky Med helicopter. Without knowing it, the group had helped Gina achieve her initial aim without encountering further opposition, resistance, or procrastination from the Trio. Almost without realising it, they had agreed that arrangements be made for a northern service to commence operation on October 1, 2007. Its operational base, again dictated by Global Helicopters Ltd, was to be at the small airfield in Colemar, a good central position from which to cover the whole of Cymran's northern half.

With regard to the group's insistence that they be allowed to nominate a Trustee, Gina had to acknowledge that she was a little uneasy from a fear that again it could set a precedent. Against this, she had weighed the chance of having a northern ally so that hopefully her voice against the Trio might not always be so lonely. Thus, in view of the latter possibility she had decided that, although the matter of setting a precedent could not be ignored, she would do nothing more than mention it and the possible consequences.

Two people had put their name forward to the fund - raisers and much to the surprise of their committee, the successful candidate was not the female considered favourite but a Colin Toben. The defeat of the favourite had disappointed Tony just as much as it had Gina. He had declared so fervently to her: "Please, I beg, let them not get to him." Silently, but equally as passionately, Gina had made the same plea. Very disappointedly, and unexpectedly, over time that forlorn hope had been eroded, though Tony never witnessed what he would have described as Colin's 'betrayal'.

Chapter 16

Tony had never before so openly expressed his unease with regard to the Trio. His wish regarding Colin Toben had revealed so much. Certainly, Gina had been aware that Tony never deferred sycophantically to her fellow Trustees, which she had concluded was yet another reason why the Trio still ignored his creditable work in raising funds. In her own case, she had considered the total lack of plaudits was due to a strong chauvinistic trait very prevalent amongst men born in the South of Cymran. This attitude Gina had attributed to the area's once thriving past when heavy industry predominated and menfolk ruled. In fact, this macho characteristic both shocked and embarrassed professional men new to the island. Laughingly, Greg had teased Gina often that she had to learn 'to know her place', while in reality the very thought angered him especially when displayed by educated men who should have known better.

Tony's antipathy to the Trio did not dampen his enthusiasm for his work. The prospect of ensuring the network of support which Gina had worked hard to establish in the North, thrived and expanded, excited him as did the agreement to have a Northern Fund Manager and a Northern Office. Agreement for both had been reached with surprising ease. The Trio had seemed to be eager to impress following receipt of the £150,000.

Thus, grabbing the opportunity before any change of heart, Tony had found suitable premises on the outskirts of Mulden, the largest town in the North. Then, following a proper appointment process, Tony, Gina and Colin Toben, the new Trustee, all believed they had chosen an excellent candidate.

Megan Carr, a woman in her mid-thirties had the qualifications, enthusiasm and personality to be a Fund Manager. Furthermore, through a family experience, she genuinely appreciated the value of the Service the Charity sponsored. In taking up her post, she had wasted no time in getting the Northern Office up and running and within a couple of weeks she had found two valuable new sponsors. Such had been Tony's confidence in Meg's ability and understanding of the office systems used that he had felt able to return to the South, and his work there just two weeks after she had started work. This had been a great relief because his loyal southern team had been informing him of their unease and puzzlement that something 'shifty' was going on! During his absence, two of the Trio, namely Marcus and Felix, had made three visits, each time accompanied by a woman introduced as Mrs Rissa Lancie. They had been given no explanation for the visits nor why this Mrs Lancie was with them though her questions had made them speculate it might be some kind of inspection.

The Monday Tony returned, however, all had been revealed when the three made their fourth visit. Rissa Lancie *had agreed* to become Fund Manager, South. Almost immediately this new appointee had announced quite calmly; "There will have to be some reorganisation to provide me with a suitable office. The two men who will deliver my personal office furniture will help with moving things and don't worry about the cost, I'm paying."

Tony and his staff had confessed to Gina that they had been rendered truly speechless, while their anger fumed within.

From hearing of the appointment from Tony and the account of Rissa Lancie's behaviour, Gina had felt very uncomfortable. "I felt so inept and powerless, especially when I was asked what was going on. Neither Colin, nor myself, had been informed, let alone consulted and our anger made no difference. Quite rightly, Tony had complained that it undermined all three of us if the Trio could do things on an 'ad hoc' basis according to their whim. We all deserved better respect and treatment, especially Tony who had to work with Rissa Lancie. Poor Tony, I really felt his pain! That last word is perhaps an unfortunate choice."

From the sigh Gina had uttered, it had been clear that her frustration prevailed regarding how helpless she had been to stop, or even put a brake on, what she described as 'dictatorial or tyrannical actions' by Marcus with the support of his two cronies. Her plea for advice from the Council of Charities had yielded nothing except a statement that the matter did not fall within the scope of its powers!

"As it stands, the Council of Charities is useless. It has no teeth" Gina had uttered angrily; the futility of the situation she had been in being felt all over again. "Do you know that just yesterday, in the 'Cymranus Mail', there was an article on the very subject stating that the Council is failing to regulate Charities effectively. It emphasised that it was not tackling the most serious abuses *AND 'Gross mismanagement'*. Damn it! I have said this in as many ways as I know how to try and get something done. On three separate occasions, I lobbied various members of the Legislative Assembly pleading for action, giving reasons as to why. I met with sympathy but nothing was ever done. Even this condemning article, outlining what is happening through lack of proper regulation, I doubt will achieve more than sympathy and promises. Oh! How I wish to be wrong."

"It really does tear at you, that's very obvious," Maxim had observed feeling very sorry for her frustration which after all her efforts she did not deserve. Over the years, there had been plenty of occasions when questionable activities within Charities across the island had raised a cry for better regulation but the fervour for reform had never managed to be strong enough for the Legislature to bring about change.

"Maybe the time has come when action can't be avoided," saying which Maxim had produced the article to which Gina had referred. Immediately she had noticed the following sentence had been underlined: '*It is despicable to think anyone can, and would, abuse charity donations for personal gain.*'

In confirming that he, too, had seen the article, Simon had added a comment directed at Maxim, which said 'and quite timely'. Naturally having heard this aside, Gina had begged to be told what made the piece so relevant. While doing so, she had appreciated that whatever all four knew would not be shared until she had finished her summary. While accepting this, she had challenged that she expected some good and constructive news when her tale was finished. Looking at the faces of all four she had been given no sign to boost her hope, that is until Pierre gave her an encouraging wink.

Chapter 17

The appointment of Colin Toben as a Trustee had led Gina to hope for an improvement in the way Charity was overseen and governed. With Damon Long absent from the first Board meeting Colin attended, leaving just two of the Trio with whom to deal, she had been bold enough to put forward a 'daring proposal'. This had suggested that an induction programme be arranged for Colin but to make it worthwhile all Trustees should attend. Hurrying on, she had turned to Felix to express an assumption that, with his legal background, he would know of a suitable expert to lead and advise on the role and responsibilities of Trustees, and to discuss the question of governance and management. Whilst the tightening faces of Marcus and Felix had indicated she had crossed the line, she had included the final sentence just to irritate them further.

"I think we would all benefit greatly," she had uttered cheerfully turning towards Colin. "You will see that we all have so much to learn still."

Before the other two, temporarily tongue-tied through shock could erupt, Colin had expressed his enthusiastic support for the proposal. His wholehearted endorsement of the idea had the effect of further fanning the seething rage with which Marcus and Felix viewed the suggestion. However, as Colin was attending his first meeting, his 'faux pas' of endorsing the idea was pardoned. With Felix ranting at Gina, the condescending and insulting tone of the pardon was not appreciated by Colin, especially as Marcus began demanding an immediate apology from Gina. In comparison to the tirade which erupted from Felix, Marcus' displeasure had seemed quite mild. Indeed, the tone, language and insults spouted by Felix even forced Marcus to adjourn the meeting very abruptly.

His action had not abated Felix's anger and cornered by him Gina had to endure all his pent up spleen. Only when he detailed for the umpteenth time his legal expertise had Gina been prompted to make any response, the opportunity arising quite conveniently for her when her assailant gave her a chance through a fit of spluttering. Managing to make her escape as Felix coughed and choked, she had reminded him that others had qualifications better than his. Whether anything she had said had been heard by him she had continued to doubt.

"Do you know?" she had stated with a cynical laugh. "If I had professed to be better qualified than any of the Trio put together, he would have gone berserk… that is, more so, and had a fit. Maybe I should have," she had mused before becoming very serious again. "His display of temper should never have been seen in a grown man, and a professional one at that." In giving her judgement, Gina had not tried to hide her contempt for the man, a disgust which had been shared at the time by Colin and Tony who had witnessed the scene with absolute disbelief.

Felix's behaviour had been so disgraceful that it had compelled Marcus, as Chairman, to apologise to Gina for his friend's splenetic outburst. Yet, though uttered with great concern and supposed sincere sympathy with the unhappy and uncalled-for situation she had suffered, Gina had known that not a word had been truly meant. Within it, Marcus had managed to reiterate that her motion had been 'out of order' but that it would be forgiven and forgotten because 'we're all good chaps here'.

Even recalling the phrase had made Gina cringe. It held the kernel of the stumbling block she had been trying to surmount. It had confirmed the Chairman's stance, which his cronies never questioned, namely that all should be his clones so as to 'never rock the boat'. By its very essence, the statement assumed that all, in this instance other Trustees, were people of goodwill. This inevitably meant that any potential for abuse was ignored on the premise it could not happen, not amongst 'good chaps'. In consequence, this made any challenge, or question very difficult and 'uncalled for', therefore, foolhardy if not risky.

From the start, Gina had acknowledged that speaking her mind left her exposed and with the need to do so increasing, she had been aware her vulnerability had been growing greater. Recognising this, she had tried to pick her battles carefully. This had meant that some issues had to be ignored whilst on others her dissent had to be moderated. Such an occasion had been the appointment of a further Trustee without any consultation. According to the Chairman another Board member had been needed because Damon would be unavailable for several months. 'The South must have a majority' had been Colin's cynical opinion. He had muttered much also about lack of due process! Not unexpectedly, the new appointee, Ranek Malesh, was an acquaintance of the Trio hailing from the same locality.

Ranek was a short, quite stout man, with a confident strut. He was an administrator at a Private College about which Gina had known nothing but its name. Her subsequent inquiries had not reassured her, being told that its high fees guaranteed passes! What had concerned her more than the College's dubious reputation was the nagging question of how the Trustees from the South seemed so well acquainted?

The only explanation that had seemed feasible had been membership of the same association, one which created a strong bond. She had compared the mysterious link to that of the 'Three Musketeers' in Alexander Dumas' novel; and their motto 'All for one and one for all'. It had amused Gina to make the observation that she had lacked fencing skills to stand any chance against her foes. Then there had been Rissa Lancie with whom to contend as well.

Chapter 18

From just meeting Rissa Lancie the new Fund Manager South, Gina had felt inexplicable unease and concern. She had tried to dismiss it by telling herself not to judge 'a book by its cover'. This woman, of forty something, clearly considered herself to be a siren both in the way she dressed and behaved. Her lack of an appropriate dress sense had revealed itself on all but one occasion the two had met. At one important function, Gina and Greg had been very embarrassed when they heard two comments by a group of guests not yet aware as to who Rissa was. By that time, she had got to the position she had been determined to achieve from day one namely that of General Manager. This job title had not been good enough for her, however, and she had designated herself CEO without any deference to the Trustees.

In fact, from the start, it had not taken long for Rissa, by various means, to achieve her own ends. By the end of her first month with the Charity, the office staff in the South had handed in their notice. Quickly, and unbeknown to Tony, Rissa had gained Marcus' approval for four of her nominees to replace them. On hearing of the changes and lack of any information on terms and salaries, Gina had sought the help of the Director of Finance of EST, who was still an adviser, to demand a meeting be convened to review finances. This Director had dealt with the Charity's accounts from the start, and his help and that of his department without charge, had been an invaluable bonus.

Both the Director and his colleagues had applauded Tony throughout for his meticulous account keeping and careful scrutiny of every penny spent. When complimented on this, Tony would respond by saying that raising the money was hard and he owed it to the people to ensure none was wasted. During the first three years, the financial position had been very tight. At least the Trio, like Gina, had not claimed expenses for travelling and also in Gina's case staying over in Awasnes for meetings. Tony, as previously mentioned, had imposed on his businessman father to sponsor his petrol and other expenses.

The extraordinary meeting had revealed the Charity's healthier financial position which meant that it could meet its increasing costs; whether some were justified, however, was a moot point. Neither Gina, nor Colin, had been pleased to hear that Rissa was being paid more than the Fund Manager in the North *and* as much as Tony. In addition, her nominated staff were being paid more than their predecessors. Gina had whispered to Colin that his community's donation had disappeared fast and unexpectedly it had seemed to prompt him to add his voice to the unreserved criticism the Director of Finance had aired about 'fait accompli' and lack of consultation. Very soon after this, the Director and his Department had instructions to withdraw from the unofficial arrangement of being the Charity's financial administrators.

The withdrawal of this unofficial arrangement, Gina had considered to be a serious blow and she had known its necessary termination had been connived. At least, for a while afterwards, Colin, had continued as an ally until, as Tony had feared 'they got to him'.

Suddenly, a sense of guilt had overwhelmed Gina over the fact that she had lost touch with Tony, who had been ousted very unkindly when he suffered some very nasty injuries from an attack. Technically, he had resigned appreciating that he would not be able to fulfil his brief properly while incapacitated. From a casual conversation with a nurse when she had travelled to visit him, Gina had learnt that it was his 'girlfriend' who supposedly had persuaded him to resign for his own safety. "Don't know what he sees in her. She's older and looks a tart, not what I would have thought his type at all," had been the nurse's comment, expressed out of a kind of confusion at the situation.

From the time she had heard the news that Tony had been assaulted, which significantly had come from his father not from the office in the South or Marcus, Gina had felt guilty at the very uncomfortable thoughts which had entered her mind almost instantly. These had remained and had strengthened based on what Tony had been able to recall and other information his father had given. In addition, the statement innocently given by the nurse that Tony had been persuaded to resign 'for his own safety' continued to niggle.

"Can I tell you that it was the first time I truly appreciated that knowing and proving can be two different things. A dilemma that far too often is never resolved." There had been no doubting Gina's genuine agony over the fact that it had not been possible for her to try.

Chapter 19

It had been Gina's intention merely to mention the attack on Tony just to show how it had allowed Rissa to take over. This had not been because she thought the incident unimportant, or irrelevant. On the contrary, it had raised many issues which were uncomfortable, and the crime had not been solved. For this reason, Gina had thought that to expand upon her reference to it would deflect her from the aim of keeping her background summary as brief as possible, being impatient to discover the real point of the meeting. The others, however, had been determined that Gina should recall all the details she could. Her suggestion that if they were that important, they should contact Tony had met with no response, not even that they would follow up on that later. This had surprised her but she had said nothing. Instead, with a resigned shrug she had begun to give them all the facts she knew.

"Well, it was not a random attack, nor a mugging, nor a failed break-in at Bates House. The police concluded that Tony had been the intended target. Nothing was stolen from him, and he had not been chosen at random. His attackers had been waiting for him"

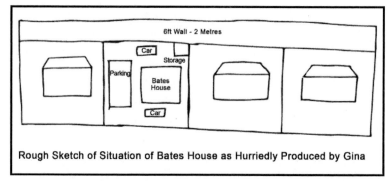

Rough Sketch of Situation of Bates House as Hurriedly Produced by Gina

Gina had been keen to stress that Tony had been leaving Bates House, where the Angelus used to have its headquarters, later than usual that evening. He had stayed late to discuss the details of an Auction a generous supporter had wished to organise to raise funds. Rissa should have been present but some domestic emergency had called her home leaving Tony to meet the donor on his own. Seemingly he had been concerned about this believing that Rissa would find some reason later to complain on the grounds that she was the Fund Manager in the South!

When the donor heard about what had happened to Tony after he had left, he had been very shocked, greatly regretting that he had not been more insistent that Tony joined him for a meal. If Tony had accepted, then the man would have had cause to wonder why Tony's car had not appeared from the back of the building to follow him to the diner. The donor's alibi and times had been checked and had been proven to be correct. His noted departure time and the time on Tony's watch, damaged in the attack, had shown that the victim's guess that he had spent some twenty-five minutes sorting out paperwork before leaving via the back door, as was his habit, had been correct.

Only Tony parked at the back of Bates House and only he left by the back door because this meant only a few strides to his car. At this point, Gina had hurried to sketch a rough plan of the site hoping that it would help. Bates House was a double fronted property of two storeys, one of six similar buildings which had been converted into office premises. The tall wall at the rear of these early 1900 dwellings belonged to an old estate, the main House of which had become a Care Home. The houses opposite were smaller, newer, lived in by respectable middle class families. Thus, the neighbourhood was pleasant and Gina had been delighted when Bates House had been offered to the Charity at a 'peppercorn' annual rent. The only drawback, on occasions, had been parking, in that the place only had the space for six vehicles: one at the front, one at the back and four to the left hand side of the building, there being only a narrow pathway along the gable end on the right. Still Trustees, and other visitors, had never faced difficulty finding a place to park on the road outside. In the evening, the road was well lit, quiet, with very little traffic.

Passing the sketch to one of the twins, Gina had sighed sadly in stating that Tony's attackers had chosen their spot well. It had allowed them the advantage of surprise and no worries about being seen, or heard. The attack had been vicious, plus there had been two against one. Such had been Tony's injuries, concussion and several fractures, he could have died, for he had lain there for hours afterwards unable to move, praying to be found.

"Let me hazard a guess as to who found him," but before Pierre had time to give a name, his brother Pascal had said it… "Rissa Lancie. Our money would be on her. Are we right?"

"No prizes for being correct," Gina had replied, "but wait for it, she found him a 5:30am in the morning. Now I bet that's a surprise."

The time, which had been quoted, had resulted in various expressions of startled puzzlement, followed by an eagerness to learn what had brought Rissa to work that early. There had been no doubting that Gina had remained unconvinced of the reason which had been given: "It would appear that Mrs Lancie had found, on arriving home the previous evening, that she had lost an expensive pendant which she had been wearing that day. Her concern and distress had been such it had led to a sleepless night until finally she had got up to look for it having become positive it had been lost in the vicinity of Bates House."

As a postscript, and with her scepticism undisguised, Gina had made it known that the pendant, of course had been found by the front door of Bates House! Furthermore, Rissa had been quick to take the credit for saving Tony's life by so providentially arriving at that early hour.

"Needless to say the Trio hailed her as a heroine. Yet there could have been so many searching questions. For instance, why did she go round to the back? She never did so during the day when at work!" Again, Gina's voice and statements had shown that her doubts and suspicions remained as strong as her anger that Tony had never received justice. The crime remained unsolved.

"Did Tony not remember anything about the attack which could have helped the Police? I take it that his assailants had their faces covered." This inquiry had come from Simon who had been right in thinking the attackers had been masked.

"They came at Tony from behind so that he had suffered a few punches before he had been able to see them. By that time, he had been on the ground being kicked. Yet he had been positive he had heard the name Clive and, even more importantly, he had insisted he had heard a woman's voice issuing a stern command: 'That's enough boys! Don't kill him'. After that he had a hazy recollection of red shoes and an anklet when the woman put a cover over him. This had been something he had repeated and repeated and kept stressing had not been a dream; but…"

"The cover?" Simon had inquired while Gina had been struggling with an irritating cough. This had been the annoying thing, no cover had been found and Rissa had sworn she had seen nothing covering Tony. Yet the Ambulance Men, and the Nurse, who attended to him first had been positive his clothes had been dry despite a spell of rain during the night.

Anticipating Simon's next query, Gina had gone on to state that the name Clive, muttered by a gruff voice, had seemed a good lead. In fact, when recovering from his surgery, Tony had become adamant that the name and the voice belonged to one of the men who had delivered Rissa's furniture. The two had a record for various misdemeanours and they worked for a female boss who had a penchant for red shoes and wore an anklet. The police would have been elated to have found concrete evidence of her involvement, being strongly suspected of using illegal activity to finance her legitimate businesses. Her alibi had been beyond reproach and that of her two employees had not been broken, while the police had lacked clues, or evidence, to bring pressure.

When all this had been related aloud, Gina had felt it sounded unreal and farfetched even though it was all true but unproven. The major stumbling block, with regard to the whole incident and Tony's recollections, had been to try and explain how a supposedly respectable, professional woman like Rissa could have known, or had any contact with people of doubtful, even unsavoury, reputation. If she had hired the two men who had delivered her office furniture to attack Tony, would that not have made her vulnerable to blackmail? This had been the issue which had stymied Gina, that is, unless there was some link. The belief that there was one had strengthened and she had wished hard that she had stumbled upon it because then the possibility of proving Rissa's involvement would become more likely. Tony and his father had never doubted that the attack had been at Rissa's behest. If she was honest, Gina knew she would have to admit that despite examining her initial assumption many times, her belief in Rissa's guilt had never weakened.

"Poor Tony! Poor Charity," she had muttered before falling into silence as she pondered again as to how an Organisation like the Angelus which did so much good, could have such ugly secrets? Once more, the phrase she had repeated to herself so often, came to mind: 'Good causes don't make people saints'. It was Maxim's voice which had brought Gina back to the present, and with a bang, when he told her that her sympathy for Tony had a sad relevance.

While she had been away, the unhappy news had been announced that Tony Rohm had died of a cerebral haemorrhage which his friends and supporters believed due to a weakness caused by his vicious beating. The words had left Gina cold, stunned and very saddened at the way Tony had been let down and forgotten so unjustly.

Chapter 20

Having given Gina the unhappy news, Maxim had considered it an opportune time to break for lunch. While the others had followed him to the dining room, Gina had taken the chance to sit quietly for a few moments to digest the final piece of information and to reflect, in general, at what had been for her an emotional morning. What she had not mentioned was that she had urged Tony to write down every single detail he remembered about the attack, to record his injuries carefully, his recovery period, after-effects and so on and to lodge this record with his father's solicitors. She had urged him to update it with anything pertinent. Thus, while sitting quietly she had prayed very fervently that he had done this so that his own words could be heard *when* the truth was uncovered.

Although Gina had cautioned herself about assuming that the blows to the head Tony had endured that fateful night had contributed to his untimely death, it would take some very strong evidence to convince her differently. Usually Gina tried to be fair and open-minded but, in this instance, she had felt no shame at her bias, and presumption. The news of Tony's death had been made more sad by the fact that she had been told he had been about to marry, that his new life in Zanlandia had been falling into place happily and well.

In leaving the Library to go to the Dining Room, Gina had heaved a heavy sigh as she voiced her thought: "Life, you do seem cruel and unfair to the wrong people." The others, on seeing her enter, had been eager to know if she was alright. Without any hesitation, she had admitted that her anger at the fact that Tony's attackers were still at liberty had increased tenfold following the news given: "If only those alibis could have been broken and I know there's a link to be found between Rissa and those people... but what?" she had exclaimed when serving herself to food from the buffet laid out for them and which had been much enjoyed by the four men.

In answer to the fear Gina had expressed that Tony's father might be prompted to act unwisely, a reassurance had been given by Simon that this was unlikely, and that Tony's parents were on an extended stay in Zanlandia getting over their loss. He had added the hope they might have some important and welcome information for them when they returned. Quietly Gina had prayed for this indeed to be so.

Over the rest of the lunch-time break, Gina had only half heard the general conversation going on around her. She had been lost in her pondering about Rissa's connection to Clive and his brother other than that she had happened to hire them to deliver her desk, etcetera. It seemed too much of a coincidence to believe that some other lout, who happened to be named Clive, with his mate, had been the attackers. The attack had been so fortuitous to Rissa's ambition, hence her absolute conviction that she had orchestrated it, because otherwise it had no purpose. That his attackers merely happened to be in the vicinity and wanted a punch-bag made no sense at all. Clive, and whoever, had been given the task but what was their connection to Rissa? If she could solve that, Gina told herself then the case would unravel. At the same time, she had recognised the need for luck.

While Gina had looked towards Rissa, the woman herself had been very keen to express the view that Tony had been attacked as some kind of message to his businessman father from some rival. The police had looked into the possibility but their line of inquiry had yielded not even a hint this could be the reason. Nevertheless, the Trio which had become a Quartet to include Ranek, had accepted Rissa's suggestion eagerly, and as fact. This had allowed them to state that, in view of 'the circumstances', Tony's resignation had to be welcomed. There had been more concern about the shock and upset suffered by Rissa in discovering the wounded Tony than there had been expressed about the unfortunate victim.

The agenda of the first meeting of the Board after the incident had included no item about the change of manager. Attempts by Gina to discuss recent changes to include the move from Bates House were thwarted. Under 'Any Other Business', she had managed to express thanks for what Tony had achieved and she had stressed the stronger financial position of Angelus was due to him. This had been endorsed by Colin who also had agreed the Minutes should include most definitely what had been said. Though agreed to, it had never come about.

The Minutes which Rissa produced became a continued source of contention on a North-South divide. At least, in this matter, Gina had never needed to take the lead though Colin had never been as heated about it at meetings as when on the phone to Gina. His excuse being it was a waste of breath. Quietly Damon would claim that this issue, like many others annoyed him also, but there was no point in annoying Marcus and Felix which was why he remained silent.

The more Gina reflected and remembered, the more bewildered she had become over her own foolishness and naivety for thinking she could have ever succeeded in directing the Board onto the path of good governance. Damon, more than once, had proffered the advice that she 'should not rock the boat while the money flowed in', the money was all that mattered. This friendly caution had been offered as part of the ethos that 'good chaps do not challenge', and that the advice should be heeded.

If Simon had not nudged Gina to say the others were back, she might have continued to sit in the Dining Room wrestling with her thoughts. To her it remained unforgiveable that 'sweet charity' had, and continued to have, a heart which had soured!

"You were thinking long and hard about something," Simon had commented, "Are you ready to share?"

"I kept feeling that I have not yet appreciated the significance of something important. That aside, do you think we can uncover facts which can't be denied, or defended, or excused?"

The questions had been asked somewhat hesitantly causing Simon to ask Gina whether something else had come into her mind.

"Not sure," she had replied. "Anyway, if a scandal is uncovered, how much harm do you think it would do?"

"It would be hoped any fall-out would be kept to a minimum. Like yourself, we would like things to change but without creating a tsunami of distrust. Ripples will have to be accepted, but small waves don't last."

This reassurance had been good to hear but it had been Simon's next statement which had cheered Gina most: "The Board of Trustees will have to stand down if…"

The mere mention of a prospect, Gina had not thought possible, had led her to interrupt excitedly.

"For that I can't wait. Please tell me the day is near."

Chapter 21

Seated once again around the table in the Library, Gina had continued her narrative without being asked, and the starting point was the takeover by Rissa. Firstly, in view of the way things had panned out later, she had thought it important, and relevant, to explain her stance, or attitude, in the difficult situation that Rissa's rise to power had presented!

"Despite the niggling worries of unease the attack on Tony had created, and his warning to watch my back, I did not greet Rissa's takeover with open antagonism although I did note it to have been 'unorthodox'. Sadly, I put my personal feelings aside because I wanted the Charity to keep on progressing. I sought to persuade myself that if the money continued to come in and lives were saved, did the murky water beneath really matter?"

During Gina's pause to reflect on yet another question which had, and still did haunt her, Simon had uttered the conclusion which she had always reached.

"But it does! It certainly does." His words uttered quietly but with feeling, showing that he had no doubts on the subject.

"That's right, it does. There's an obligation. If you know, see or hear of any wrongdoing, you have a responsibility to speak out."

Pierre pointed out that the personal cost can be high, a point on which there had been unanimous agreement. "I found it impossible to ignore the poor governance, the bad management, the lack of accountability and other concerns arising from the new management style. Constantly, and justifiably in my view, I argued that Trustees needed to know details of the working structure and other facts to be able to scrutinise and monitor. Alas, Rissa, supported by the Quartet interpreted this as unwarranted interference. I found... well... lots of things, suffice to say, I was poles apart from Rissa's management policy which was that all the Trustees needed to know was that the Charity was solvent. Everything else came under management and her jurisdiction. I shall repeat, from a distance, it soon became impossible to piece together what was going on and the office staff appointed by Rissa were never helpful or forthcoming."

To illustrate what she had said, Gina had thought a few examples necessary. A month after Rissa's rise to power, there had been a change of premises. The reason, which had been claimed, to give the staff a feeling of greater security but for all to have been arranged so quickly Gina had been convinced negotiations had been started before the attack on Tony. The single storey building, to which the headquarters had been moved, had been the abandoned premises of a building firm. There was certainly more space and ample parking but the annual rent was much higher and the area around not as good... a point emphasised a year later when another move had taken place. Far too late, Gina had discovered that the abandoned lease remained to be paid for another three years and this was not the only example of the Charity entailing continued, unnecessary costs.

In every instance, there had been some supposedly pressing reason why there had been no time for consultation with Colin and herself. When dissatisfaction was expressed Felix would always in some way remind Gina that 'good chaps accepted the judgement of others', while Damon would manage to whisper that she really should let things be.

Chapter 22

When leaving the First Board Meeting after Rissa's takeover, Colin had remarked to Gina how glad he was that Megan Carr was in charge in the North. In the next couple of months, he had repeated this during telephone conversations leaving Gina to remind him that Rissa had not yet travelled North! "You don't think she would...? No, she can't. Definitely not." After four months, however, the dreaded had happened. Unannounced Rissa had arrived at the Northern Office and before introducing herself had begun a tirade of criticism in front of members of the public. Megan Carr had complained about such behaviour and public humiliation of herself and her two members of staff. In response, Rissa had told her to apologise or leave and Megan had chosen the latter. leaving Rissa to stand at the door shouting abuse in a very fishwife manner as Megan got into her car and drove away. Needless to say, none of this got relayed South, and as she had been immediately head-hunted, Megan made no claim of constructive dismissal. The two members of staff believed the quick change of premises which followed had been necessary to avoid embarrassment after Rissa's public display!

Less than six months later another unhappy episode had happened in the North which really began the serious down-spiral in Gina's relationship with the self-styled Chief Executive, and in consequence with the Cabal. Returning from holiday, the following headline emblazoned on the front page of the 'Cymranus Mail' had caught her attention.

'Sacked at bedside of dying husband
Charity shows no compassion when loyal
Staff member undertakes vigil after
Husband's massive stroke...'

No reader could have ignored the headline nor the article, thus, not surprisingly, immediately on getting home, she had rung Anya Marley at the Northern Office where the sacked member had worked. Since Megan's departure, quietly and efficiently Anya had run the Office with one full-time and one part-time staff member. None were enamoured of Rissa, or her management style. Anya had confessed that she made herself as invisible as possible when Rissa visited but Mary, the sacked member, had often dared to challenge. To her cost, it would have seemed, in view of what happened, her absence when Rissa visited resulting in her immediate dismissal.

Before Gina's conversation with Anya ended, cryptically it had been suggested that she should check her messages. Then she had given the news that Mary's husband had died. The message referred to requested Gina to contact a named person at the Council of Charities. When she followed the instruction, she had been surprised that this man thought that she had asked to speak to him. Though this had been interesting, her main concern had been to use the opportunity to acquaint him with her many worries, of which the sacking fiasco was just one. Remembering that the Council had not fulfilled its only meaningful statutory duty, namely to visit a new Charity within three years of its establishment to review its procedures, she had urged that this be done.

"I am sure you can guess the next bit," Gina had stated with a smirk, "The Council of Charities wrote that at the behest of Mrs G. Fiddes, to fulfil its obligation, two of its staff would visit. They would want also to discuss the unfortunate headlines about which Mrs Fiddes had expressed great concern. Talk about being dropped right in it."

There had been no light-heartedness when she continued. "A letter from Marcus stated that an emergency meeting to discuss the Council's letter was to be held at a Hotel in Acron, a town roughly midway between North and South. The choice of venue should have told me that it was more than likely I would be the only one there besides Marcus and Felix and, of course Rissa, and so it proved to be. The meeting was to be an Inquisition following Rissa's accusation of interference and unjust criticism. As with the Inquisition of old, the meeting was not about fair play and justice, its purpose was to condemn."

Marcus had begun proceedings by expressing a total lack of understanding as to what had prompted Gina to contact the Council of Charities! Being corrected that it had been a request from the Council to be in contact, definitely had not been expected, nor had it suited. Felix had resorted to calling Gina a liar which Marcus, however, had insisted he retracted with an apology. His outburst and slander, though withdrawn, had prompted Gina to rile him by stating that it would appear the usually toothless and docile Council could not ignore the headlines which had drawn some justified bad publicity for which Rissa was to blame.

Immediately, Rissa had claimed her action justified and, stressing his legal background, Felix had jumped to her defence. In no way, according to him could 'wrongful dismissal', which Gina had claimed had happened, be alleged by Mary. The challenge, Gina had then issued to bet on it, had been viewed as yet another example of her rashness, foolhardiness, *and* ignorance.

Later, Gina had the satisfaction of discovering that to keep the matter out of Tribunal, a settlement with Mary had been necessary, the sum of £15,000 being paid along with a further £5000 for silence. The award might have been greater if the widowed Mary had not needed money quickly so that she accepted the first offer.

"Of course, the whole matter was never mentioned officially to the Trustees, and certainly not its cost. And no, there was never even an apology to me in private." The last statement Gina had added to forestall possible comments by the twins who had then asked about the visit by the two Officers from the Council of Charities.

The report that the two Officers had produced had recognised important key issues. It had stated that there was a great need to improve the general audit trail, the phrase 'deficient record-keeping' repeated several times and underlined. The Officers noted that they had been unable to establish evidence of any schedule of regular meetings and that it had disappointed them greatly that only Marcus and Felix had been present for their summation session. Even Damon and Ranek had gone as far as to angrily declare they had been deliberately excluded, and that it had not been due to a misunderstanding, which Marcus had claimed. In response, Marcus had expressed great sadness at seeing their anger and foolish thoughts, all arising from Gina's uncalled for contact with the Council of Charities.

"I ignored the comment and drew their attention to the one success Rissa could claim and which the Report had described as an 'excellent arrangement'. This was the tie negotiated between the Charity's Lottery 'Cymairalot' and Zanlandia State Lottery."

Gina had then explained how the scheme worked and what the benefits were, the first being that the Charity was able to use, without charge, Zanlandia's weekly numbers. To ensure the Angelus maintained its standards of supervision and management, it appointed its own people as overseers. Thus, the Cymairalot was closely and well monitored which had meant one less worry for Gina who had been very pleased the tie also kept administrative, legal and other costs to a minimum.

Sadly, Gina had to admit that the same could not be claimed for the 'in-house' raffle organised every quarter. In fact, she had been appalled when, shortly before resigning, she had discovered how badly it was administered and supervised leaving her very uneasy about the fairness of any results. The anger of Marcus and Rissa, when they found she had stumbled on the room where Viana, Rissa's P.A., dealt with the ticket stubs, had made her negative thoughts grow into real worries.

These worries she had buried, confessing that she had salved her conscience by telling it that she was seeing bogeys where there were none, and if there were, she had no chance of proving anything. Living a distance away from the headquarters at Aswanes had helped her to forget all the sorry secrets!

Chapter 23

A very short period of improvement had followed the sacking fiasco and the inspection which had followed. Before the summation meeting, a timetable had been prepared in order to show that regular meetings were always the intention. If only there had been follow-up visits by the Officers some real improvements might slowly have been achieved. Anyway, even though confirmation of the Monday Board Meeting was only issued on the Friday previous to the due date with no paperwork available beforehand, the first two meetings on the drawn up timetable had taken place as scheduled. However, as not confirmed until the last possible moment, Colin had not been able to attend either but Gina had ignored the inconvenience and attended. This would not have been possible without Greg's support and tolerance for which she knew she had never thanked him enough.

Travelling to Aswanes at short notice had presented problems to Colin on many occasions. His wife was bi-polar and when down she would not accompany him and, without company at home she could not be left. When his wife was well, they worked hard, within their locality, to keep momentum of support for the Angelus as high as when the £150,000 was raised. Thus, in view of their efforts, it had irked Colin greatly not to be informed of special events held for the Charity whether North or South of Cymran. They claimed their hard work within the locality had earned them the right to become more widely known as pillars of the organisation. It had annoyed Gina, too, on many occasions to learn of an event, held not too far away, from an account in the newspaper. There had been instances when people had expressed surprise at her non-attendance thereby missing a chance to network with beneficial results.

To receive, early in 2012, direct notification from two prestigious hotels in the North about the garden parties they were arranging to host to raise funds had been a greatly appreciated gesture. It had allowed her to inform Colin and get him an invitation for which his wife had been exceeding grateful. With great relish she had stated that it felt good to get one over on those in the South who had told them nothing as usual. This sentiment Gina had shared. To attend the first, she and Greg had stayed overnight at a nearby hotel to avoid an early start, which Colin and his wife had faced. Consequently, it had not pleased them to discover Marcus, Felix, Damon and Rissa had enjoyed overnight hospitality at the venue. With regard to the latter some very unflattering remarks had been heard and such had been the disapproval of a group of influential ladies they had sought out Gina to inform her their generosity had been tempered as a result. In fact, they had urged Gina to have a word with Rissa on the matter 'of her attire'.

"No doubt, you rushed to do so," Pascal had commented, before stating that they had become aware, at first hand, of some of the unfavourable comments Rissa's dress sense occasioned, a remark Gina had found interesting but had let ride.

Continuing to the second Garden Party held a month later, Gina mentioned that she had been disappointed that Colin had not been able to attend. More of a surprise had been that she was the only Trustee present but that Rissa was there with all four of the staff from the Southern Office. They had all travelled separately and were to enjoy the Hotel's hospitality for two nights, all happy revealed to Gina by one of the entourage. This kind of imposition made Gina seethe inwardly while outwardly she had been full of smiles as she mingled amongst the guests glad at least that there should be no complaints about Rissa's clothing on this occasion. On the contrary, she had been uncharacteristically staid in what she was wearing.

"While circulating, I saw a man in his fifties standing on his own and seemingly agitated, constantly looking at his watch. Intrigued, I approached him but before I managed a greeting, he introduced himself as the 'Northern President of the Angelus Charity.' My jaw literally dropped as he told me he was waiting for his wife with whom I must work as he had noticed me being very busy networking and he would report favourably on this."

While making the statement Gina had watched the expressions of each of her listeners carefully and, without exception, all had shown disbelief at what they were hearing. They had been as much at a loss for words as she had been at the time. Not that the said gentleman had noticed her silence and shocked expression straight away and when he did, he had presumed it was because it was dawning on her that he had been a sports commentator and pundit. "After that comment, I know I stood there agape not knowing whether to laugh or cry!"

"Who was the idiot?" Maxim inquired, far from amused by what he heard. "I hope you managed to deflate his ego and that you corrected him on his false assumptions."

"Ifan Behn, the name genuinely meant nothing to me."

"Oh him!" Simon spat out, his disgust and low opinion clear without any further words though he had gone on to inform Gina that Ifan Behn's pomposity, self-importance and lack of tact had been responsible for ending his media career almost as soon as it had begun.

"When I told him I was a founding Trustee, he made no comment. Actually, I did wonder if he knew what the term meant. Still, saying that, I can name others similarly challenged!" the sarcasm being well appreciated by her audience of four. For a moment, it had lightened her sad chronicle of farce and failure. There were, of course, so many lovely things she could recount from the army of volunteers who, in all weathers, worked tirelessly to raise funds. They and the donors deserved so much better from the top, namely a greater respect for their efforts with no advantage taken. It had been to try and protect them that she had continued, that is until…

Carrying on after the brief pause, Gina had told how before she had been able to move away from the pompous Mr. Behn, his wife had arrived breathless and clearly irritated. Her intention of making a grand entry by helicopter had been foiled, its on-line duties had taken priority! This had meant that she had been forced to drive herself to the venue to arrive hassled and late. "That damned emergency spoiled everything," her angry verdict uttered before she noticed Gina's presence nearby because she had turned to speak to one of the Hotel's staff.

Although they had not met before, Gina had seen her photograph in the paper when it noted, soon after her appointment as Fund Manager North, the opening of a new Warehouse in Drafon from which new and second-hand goods would be sold in aid of the Charity. Gina's attention had been drawn to the coverage by a fuming Colin who like herself had known nothing about the Grand Opening nor anything about the new appointment. The latter had upset Anya as well when she read about it in the newspaper. She had phoned Gina to inquire whether the North was to have two offices or was the one she worked at to be closed. Her anger and question had been justified but Gina had no idea how to answer her query, which Anya had well appreciated.

"Rhyane Behn had known who I was but the way she looked at me should have warned me that I was not greeting a friend. Furthermore, what I went on to say was reported to Rissa as unforgiveable criticism."

Hearing this, Maxim had asked, if it was supposedly so terrible should she be repeating it to her listeners' tender ears? "Brace yourself," Gina had responded in a similar mocking tone. "My 'faux pas' was to mention that I had been sorry to miss her when I called in at the new warehouse, and the office within it, on two occasions hoping to say 'hello'. Still, I had been able to meet her assistant Linda and others which had been good. What I said, alas and woe is me etcetera, Rhyane viewed as criticism of her absence. Not the intention at the time but…?"

Despite the time which had elapsed since the unhappy scene which followed, Gina's puzzlement remained undiminished. Some twenty minutes after her brief introduction to Rhyane Behn an angry Rissa, with a weepy Rhyane and husband Ifan in tow, had accosted her demanding to know why she had been so rude and critical of poor Rhyane! "I was dumbfounded. The verbal attack was so full of nonsense, I was on the verge of real, not false, tears, when a voice demanded the untrue accusations should stop. It was good to have a defender but it did seal my fate."

The man whispered something to Ifan Behn after which he and the two women left, seemingly temporarily bruised, their plan having failed. Stunned by the episode, Gina had not been quick enough to get the defender's name before he rushed towards someone beckoning at him from a distance. In departing, he had warned her that the Behns were not trustworthy, a matter of fact not hearsay. Although Gina had tried to seek him out afterwards she had not succeeded nor even managed a name. Her Sir Galahad appeared to have disappeared back to Camelot.

Chapter 24

The last chapter in the annals of Gina's association with the Angelus was that which angered, saddened and hurt her most. Her first encounter with Rhyane Behn had served well to show her character so that when complaints came her way about the new Fund Manager North, Gina had found no reason to doubt their validity. Such had been the quick rise of dissatisfaction amongst the volunteers that they had written to express their views but no reply had been received from the Chairman.

Not replying to correspondence had been a theme Gina had needed to address on numerous occasions. The lack of courtesy applied not only to complaints but to generous donations as well as invitations. With regard to the latter even the Consul for the South West Region of Cymran had found it necessary to telephone Gina, with whom he was acquainted, to express his displeasure at being ignored. A gift of £50,000 had been diverted to another deserving cause through rudeness on the part of Marcus and the office in Aswanes. An invitation delivered to Marcus' home address had not been acknowledged and neither had he attended the function to which he had been asked, hence the loss of the donation. Very scathingly the Consul had expressed his opinion of Marcus by saying that the behaviour was only to be expected from an 'Aswanes Jack'. This had been a term Gina had not heard before but allegedly it was stated to be the reason he had been blackballed by reputable organisations and clubs. From what had been disclosed, Gina had decided the term applied to a chancer, an upstart who had gained no real polish but believed he had.

At the next meeting of the Board, Gina had discovered that the strong and widespread wave of dissatisfaction and anger amongst volunteers, of which she had become aware, was more than warranted. Very proudly Rissa had announced that sixteen Executive Fund Raisers had been employed, each on a salary of £18,000, a detail she omitted. The appointments had meant that a sizeable number of volunteers had been told by email their services were no longer required. These emails had included no word of thanks for invaluable support over the years.

"I felt their hurt, their betrayal. My anger was not tempered when I questioned the validity of the appointments entailing a substantial, unnecessary, and costly change undertaken without consultation. The use of the term 'Executive', I also viewed as inappropriate and I was flabbergasted to hear Felix express agreement on this point... but it was only a momentary slip."

These Fund Raisers had been given no target amounts to achieve which Gina had openly considered ludicrous. Too late, she had found that out after a year in the post, each had cost an additional £11-£13,000 in travelling expenses and the amount that they *might have* generated fell far too short of their overall cost.

"That bad?" Simon had asked.

"Very definitely," the thought of this wasted expenditure still angered her. "My questioning of Rissa's action led to the expected rude, personal tirade, followed, on this occasion, by her tearful exit. Damon had then expressed his frustration and anger at my insistence on upsetting people! Rissa's appointments could be afforded because the public always met the increasing sum needed by the organisation and that was all that mattered. His record seemed stuck on this point and this caused me to demand detailed and comprehensive accounts to be made available without fail in advance of the next meeting which should be held within six weeks. This demand was seconded by Colin and that there should be no prevarication on the matter."

According to what had been later sworn to be the truth, Rissa's absence from work for a couple of weeks after this had been necessitated by the emotional distress which Gina had caused her. The real truth was different, namely a planned two weeks' holiday period while the subsequent absence had occurred due to some worrying family problems. Thus, in view of such circumstances and the lack of clarity regarding what was happening, Gina and Colin had felt it safe to assume that neither the extra meeting nor that scheduled for a month later which was to include the AGM would actually happen. The lack of advanced papers which they had requested had made them confident in their assumption. It had come as a shock, therefore, to hear that the two meetings had taken place but that due to no one from the North being present, the AGM had been postponed.

Details of the new date, venue and agenda for the AGM when they did arrive, had given Gina just three days' notice. Only on contacting Colin who had claimed he had received nothing, not even by email, had she decided she would travel South. Greg had been keen for her to show that she had not been cowed by all the 'slings and arrows' and to see if they would dare to try and oust her, a step he had always argued they greatly feared to take.

To make the journey worthwhile, AGM's usually being very short, they had decided to travel on the Saturday for the Monday meeting and return on the Tuesday. The hotel in Fridcar where they had stayed was situated in its own grounds on the north-eastern boundary of the city. Moreover, it was only a mile from Cymran's Sports Council Complex in whose Board Room the AGM was to take place. However, during the weekend neither the Charity nor anything related to it, had been mentioned, both Gina and Greg had determined to have a quiet, pleasant time in each other's company after some hectic weeks.

On the Monday morning, Gina had woken early and immediately had felt an overwhelming sense of foreboding. Still, she had waved cheerily when she set off at 10:30am for the eleven o' clock start, but had responded to Greg's wish of 'good luck' that she would definitely have need of it. Following instructions given at the reception, Gina had found the Board Room easily. Its door opened to the right so she had not been able to see the table at which the gathered group had been seated until she stepped beyond it. Then it had been clear that a meeting was already in progress.

"It's not even eleven, so why has the AGM started early?" she had asked in all innocence, somewhat startled by the scene. Loudly, hysterically, Rissa had screamed a response:

"Did I not say Gina would claim she knew nothing about this meeting? Did I not say she would attend only the AGM?"

Other utterings had followed from Marcus and Felix expressing concern about Rissa and cursing Gina's insistence on causing her grief. If the paramedic Co-ordinator had not indicated an empty chair by him, Gina would have turned and left. Instead as calmly as possible, she had made her way to the place indicated. On sitting, she had seen written on his papers: 'Ignore them. Hang in there. Meeting started at 10 am. M. F. D. R were in private session with Rissa prior to that!' There was such shouting and chaos that Gina had doubted if anyone had noticed her reading the note. To resume order, an irritated Carl – the paramedic – had thumped the table and boomed: "Mr Chairman restore order now. I have work to which I must rush back."

In the shocked silence which ensued, Gina had grabbed the opportunity to state:

"I want everyone to know I was not informed of any other meeting, or meetings, except for the AGM to start at eleven. It would be madness to travel South, spend money to stay, and then not attend what else had been arranged."

"You're mad and a liar, I believe Rissa and not you." This yelled declaration had come from Felix who in his wimpish, sycophantic way had been patting Rissa's hand as she resumed her sobbing.

"Everyone has witnessed Felix's statement. It amounts to slander. I shall expect you to clearly remember his words, uttered deliberately to malign and without any just cause."

At this point, Rissa and Felix at her heels, had rushed out only to re-enter seconds later.

"What was that all about?" Carl had whispered pushing his papers over to Gina to show there was one item left. Scanning through the paper, Gina had spotted some glaring mistakes which when proceedings resumed, she had stated invalidated it. Without hesitation Damon had proposed its deferral to the next meeting to allow time for a fuller, accurate submission. All had nodded agreement which Gina had believed stemmed from an eagerness to move on and avoid further eruptions. There was, however, to be one more.

The next 'lava spill,' Gina had incited very deliberately. This had not been hard. She had merely pointed out that the agenda for the AGM once again omitted to include the election of Chairperson and Deputy. Hurrying to put her point over, she had stated that to presume both incumbents wished to continue in office yet further, beyond the constitutional terms, showed a lack of courtesy as well as due diligence by Fellow Trustees. In previous years, her reference to the omission had always been ignored but not on this occasion. A fuming Marcus had exploded to declare that he and Felix planned to continue in office for several more years and that Gina was in a minority to think otherwise! Not yet cowed, Gina had demanded that the Minutes, when written noted verbatim what Marcus had stated. After this, the rest of the brief agenda had been nodded through with great haste. Battle weary, all Gina had wanted was to make her escape, the feelings of despondency and helplessness weighing heavily upon her.

Departing alongside Carl, she had been waylaid by Marcus who, having donned his guise of charm, wanted *as Chairman* to introduce her to the two new Trustees, seemingly approved before the AGM. Eagerly he had stressed his success in gaining the interest of two such talented men who would be such an asset. Politely, when acknowledging them, Gina had expressed her very sincere hope that they understood their role and the necessity for good governance. Without appreciation of this and the careful scrutiny the role of Trustees demanded, abuses inevitably occurred and more seriously when unchecked. After this, she had turned and left, ignoring the buffet which had been provided courtesy of the Sports Council and towards which the others had hurried.

Chapter 25

The drive back to the Hotel had seemed to Gina more like ten miles and not just one due to hold-ups and traffic queues. Just seeing Greg would lift her heart and he was always such a good listener and she had much to pour out. However, immediately on seeing him she had known something was wrong, he had lost his usual vitality and good humour. Only later, after a quiet, but pleasant afternoon followed by a lovely dinner, did he admit that he had a continuing and uncomfortable pain in his back. Once back home, he had sought medical opinion which revealed a serious aortic aneurism. Without delay, he had entered Hospital to undergo the lengthy surgery which he had survived, leading Gina to comfort herself that the worst part was over and her Greg had defied the odds. Then, much to her despair, complications had occurred which the medical team failed to resolve.

Three weeks after their trip to Fridcar, Greg was dead. Reflecting on Gina's account of the meeting, her lovely husband had remarked that, if people of supposed standing behaved so badly, so continuously, it was becoming a world in which he loathed to live. "Where's that desert island we can escape to?" he had asked, his smile and good humour returning. Even so, Gina remained saddened by this despairing comment and the thought that the trip to Fridcar had robbed him of his optimism and will to fight.

Four days after Greg's funeral, Gina who had not been feeling at all well had found out the reason why. With a vengeance, she had succumbed to shingles and, worst of all, the area of eruption was the right side of her face and head. Luckily, on the morning the outburst had burst forth, she had struggled to answer the persistent ringing of the doorbell. She had been aware that her face was swollen and that only her left eye allowed her limited vision, so not a pretty sight to greet any caller. To hazily see it was Petra, had overwhelmed Gina with joy, so much so, that she had collapsed into her arms.

For the next five days, Petra had been her nurse and constant attendant but Gina had little recall of these days, except for the discomfort, because of a high fever. The young lady Doctor had been so worried about Gina's right eye that she had sought expert opinion and help for which Gina had cause to be forever grateful. According to Petra, there had been one consolation to her very poorly period and eyes too swollen to open, it was that she had not been able to see herself. Seemingly, Gina had looked like someone who had gone through a car windscreen. Still, for weeks, the evidence had remained.

During Gina's days of incapacity, Colin had phoned, leading Petra to tell him that her patient was really poorly. He had informed Petra that it was more likely due to verbal attacks suffered than the shock of Greg's death. Having met each other at Greg's funeral, from what Petra had afterwards let slip, Gina had good reason to believe the conversation had been long and informative. Certainly, it had been informative enough for Petra to deal sharply with Marcus when he phoned suggesting that, in view of Greg's death, the shock resulting in Gina's subsequent illness, he would understand completely if she wanted to resign.

A month later, Marcus had telephoned again, on this occasion to hope Gina would be well enough to attend a meeting at Tralyn the following week. The agenda, he had stressed, included matters on which she had sought discussion and so was very much worth the effort to attend. With such a carrot having being dangled, although far from recovered and with her face and right eye still bearing evidence of their recent ordeal, she had travelled to Tralyn. In fact, to avoid an early start, she had stayed overnight at a Hotel in the town not too far from the College where the meeting was to be held. She had arrived at the venue at the same time as Colin who had been solicitous in his inquiries about her health. Yet, not one member of the Quartet had inquired how she had been faring nor did any of the four offer condolences. The two new Trustees were absent and the Charity's Accountant merely managed a nod. Gina had to admit that the lack of common decency had hurt especially as she had been dressed in black, deliberately to remind. Still, for once, the discussions had been constructive and a clear forward strategy had been hammered out without too much angst. Nevertheless, she had not been confident that it would be adhered to, rather she had believed it all to have been a token exercise. This had stemmed from the fact that Rissa had not been present to voice objection.

At the start, it had been stated that Rissa was on a two week much needed holiday. When it came to Any Other Business however, Marcus had distributed a copy of a letter, written by Rissa, demanding Gina's resignation. If this did not happen then she would have to leave the Charity, leaving it crippled without her. The keys to power were hers, she had overall control having fought fiercely against any 'power sharing'. The stunned silence and reaction of others had indicated that they had received no advance notice of the bombshell. Marcus meanwhile distributed a copy of his reply to Rissa's missive, received he had said only the previous day. Immediately, Gina had pointed out that his statement did not tally with the dates on both letters. In addition, she had described Rissa's demand and threat not hers to make and yet Marcus, in his reply, had indicated that he was very happy to succumb to her ransom demand.

"When I asked Marcus where was justice when he had made himself judge and jury, he had spluttered that I could avoid further heartache if I stepped down. Before I could reply, Damon rushed to suggest the investigator used by a notable firm of Solicitors be employed to mediate. The others chorused their support for the proposal urging Marcus to agree after which he closed the meeting and everyone scurried away as if I had become invisible."

Some weeks later the investigator referred to had contacted Gina and, as she was to be in Fridcar on business, she had agreed to meet him at the Hotel at which she was to stay. Her agreement had been prompted by curiosity but when they did meet, she had been impressed by his professionalism. After half an hour of general chat, he had spent an hour scanning through Gina's dossier of letters to Marcus following meetings reiterating her points and comments and recording the responses and the harsh criticisms to which she had been subjected. No replies had ever been received even though she had stated that this meant the contents had been accepted as correct. This was a point

Gina had emphasised to the Investigator who listed for her all the people he had spoken to in person and those with whom it had been a telephone conversation.

Days later when she arrived home, Gina had found a message to ring the Investigator as soon as possible and this she had done. His news had not been good. He had submitted his report which exonerated her completely of the charges Rissa had made. The report, however, had been rejected outright because its intended brief had been to crucify Gina. The man had admitted to her his bewilderment and total disgust at such dishonourable behaviour. His verdict that the 'knives are out' had not come as a surprise, nor in a way, had been the next piece of news given by Marcus over the phone. This had been that he had to hand a very condemning report written by the replacement woman mediator!

"When I asked for a copy, he refused firstly on the grounds it would be hard for me to read how everyone hated me, nevertheless, I insisted and stated that legally it could not be denied me. Now the author I never did meet, or speak to, and yet the report stated differently. For instance, on the day we supposedly met in Strwyth, I could prove I was in Zanlandia. Rhyane Behn's hearing is so good that at a distance over two hundred miles away, she heard me abusing Rissa at meetings. I do have a copy and it is worth reading, being so full of blatant and farcical falsehoods. Even Marcus had to acknowledge, knowing I had seen it, that it contained some 'unfortunate, ridiculous allegations' not that this made one iota of difference."

In the post, a week later, Gina had received an injunction forbidding her from speaking to anyone about the Charity. Even the local press had received a warning that if Gina approached with a story nothing was to be

112

printed. As it happened, two days before receiving the injunction, Gina had discovered that Rhyane had allowed thirty friends to attend a £100 a ticket Charity Function for free. This information had been given to Gina by the not very happy owners of the large Manor House where the prestigious evening had taken place. Such had been the behaviour of Rhyane and friends particularly that of a very drunk Rhyane, that Gina had felt obliged to visit the owners to apologise in person to them and their staff. So great had been their disgust at the behaviour that she had begged the Council of Charities to take some action. The answer she had received had been one that she had expected, namely that more likely it would be claimed that Rhyane's generosity had been given retrospective approval by the Chairman, especially as the sum was just £3000!

When the injunction had been received, Gina had almost conceded to Marcus' behest to resign but she had decided to hang on to frustrate and annoy the Quartet. This, she knew, would make it difficult for Marcus to hold any meeting until the next AGM. During this time, she had determined to hound the Accountant to give her detailed accounts. When he finally acceded and gave her most of what she had requested, she had found many anomalies even he could not explain, though he had tried without success!

It would have been easy to resign by letter but Gina had decided she wanted to look each in the eye as she made the following statement:

"Nothing prepares you for the loss of a loved one and someday it will happen to you. At the time you will expect sympathy and compassion which none of you extended to me. Instead, you resorted to risible lies and tried to discredit me. Why? What is the great fear? One day it will be revealed, along with the great injustice I suffered. I plead that you all appreciate that good governance and due diligence are duties you owe a generous public."

On finishing, she had walked out. No one had followed and no letter had been written subsequently to thank her for all of her efforts and generosity over the years. This had not surprised her but it had hurt. "It said such a lot about the quality of the people with whom I had tried to work," Then, feeling great relief that her very sad and disheartening narrative had reached its end, Gina had added an impish post script.

"I have described the *good* intent and the wonderful work of the volunteers and the Sky Med Paramedics, as well as the *bad* governance and its consequences. Now it's your turn to reveal just how ugly and pervasive the cancer at the heart of the organisation really is, for I do believe you have found some despicable facts. This meeting is not about the million, though it definitely should be repaid. Come, it's time you told me the point of this meeting."

Chapter 26

Despite Gina's plea on concluding her summary to hurry and tell her what they had discovered, the others had imposed on her patience by declaring it a good time to have a short break. Actually she had appreciated the opportunity to go out on to the veranda where she hoped the air might blow away some of the mire with which, by association, she had become tarnished. She could not shake herself free of collective responsibility for whatever wrong that there was to be revealed.

Within a few minutes, Maxim had joined her, eager to know she was alright. Then, after telling her the others were enjoying tea and Jane's fruit cake he had asked:

"Why did you never mention all the personal attacks? You expressed concerns but you never admitted the serious depths of your worries. Why was that? Why did you not confide in me fully?"

His question was a very fair one. Actually, she had felt guilty almost continuously for not revealing to him the unadulterated truth.

"Misplaced pride," she had answered. "I hoped against hope that things would change, naïve fool that I was. Also, all I had was a feeling of unease, mainly that the possibilities were there. I had no proof, so why spoil an illusion? The outer façade was great; lives were being saved. How often do families put on a good front, seem pillars of society, while jealousy, strife and cruelty dominates behind closed doors? So yes I tempered the truth for the greater good. Oh! Doesn't that sound hollow!"

Simon, who had come out to say that he and the twins were ready to continue, having heard some of what she had said, commented that she should not condemn herself. "On all levels you and the cabal were no more alike than chalk and cheese. Believe me, you were the valuable, the others the worthless counterfeit as you will soon see."

Her humour restored by this, she had joked that she was undecided as to what cheese she would be. Thus, she had been smiling broadly when they re-entered the Library and seeing the bemused expressions of the twins, she had whispered she would share the joke with them later.

Once seated, it had been Simon, on a nod from Maxim, who had begun proceedings. In a very judicial tone, he had asked Gina if she knew anything about the K3?

"Now I've heard of K9, of course, who hasn't? Then there is the Italian organisation P2, but no, K3 means nothing to me." The rather flippant tone of her response, she had regretted immediately especially as she recalled that Trevor Mason had mentioned K3 through being fearful a newly appointed Non-Executive Director of EST might be a member. He had described it as a 'mafia-like organisation found in the South' of whose members one should be wary. Simon confirmed K3 was a southern organisation found in the three largest conurbations Fridcar, Aswanes and Barport. "Now you wondered how your southern Trustees knew one another

116

and quoted Dumas' Musketeers being 'all for one and one for all' and you were right to do so. K3, which is a far more secretive fellowship than the Masons, expects its members to look out for each other and help one another to seek advancement by fair or other means." Hearing all this had made the pieces of her jigsaw lodge into place in a way Gina had imagined but had never before been able to position with certainty.

Reference had then been made to two of Gina's statements relating to Marcus, based on what the Consul had confided. Men who were chancers, or whose dubious character had caused other organisations to blackball their membership, were just the kind of people K3 welcomed. Others were ensnared because of the positions they held. In short, the respectability, or 'standing' of those who belonged to K3 was questionable.

"Help!" Gina had exclaimed, "I think you are going to reveal more serious, unsavoury truths than I ever expected. Optimistically, I hoped that my detested Trio which became a cabal of four, was guilty only of gross ineptitude rather than serious malicious misbehaviour. Regarding Rissa and her staff buddies, including Rhyane, though it grieves me to admit it, I have long expected bad news, and yet not too bad, a vain hope perhaps."

Looking at the twins, Gina could see that they were agog to reveal the results of their investigative work but before handing over to them, Simon had been very keen to stress that the task undertaken by the Niven twins and their co-investigators, had not been an easy one, quickly accomplished. This Gina could well appreciate. What, she wondered, might Marcus, Felix, Damon and Ranek not have wished to be known? The twins had seemed disappointed that she had offered no guess when asked by them to put forward her thoughts as to what Marcus' secret might be. At the same time, they had been happily confident no guess would have been right.

"Marcus has two wives. His other wife lives in Zanlandia. He's a bigamist."

This news Pierre had blurted bluntly, being then keen to emphasise that living a double life needed talents Gina might not have imagined Marcus to have, and this was true. "He is also a fraudster" Pascal had added. "Along with his brother and others, he runs a company which operates 'piggy back' on the resources of the Company for which he and his brother and the two others work. All very cleverly done, under the radar so to speak and very profitable."

This pattern of each contributing in turn had continued when giving their information on each of the others. At least with regard to Felix, Gina found that she had been right in thinking the dominance of his mother, to whom he had to kowtow probably explained his frustration and petulant temperament when out of her reach. This was a parent who expected him to deny his inclinations and vow celibacy which she had guessed had been what made him a candidate for K3. What Gina had not known was that Felix was the Company Secretary to Trygana Products, namely Marcus' profitable 'side-line' firm. On hearing that Felix had been embroiled, she had jumped ahead and guessed that it was very likely that Damon, too, would have some connection. On first meeting him, she had been told that he and Marcus had met through being members of the same flying club. The twins confirmed this and told Gina that, until Marcus qualified as a pilot, it had been Damon who had flown him over to Zanlandia. They were unable to say if he knew about Marcus' other family. In any case, in Pierre's opinion, it was an acquaintanceship and not friendship! Finally, according to Pascal, it would appear that Damon had worked hard to clear his brother-in-law of an allegation of rape. The girl had disappeared and the charge had been dropped. Consequently, it would seem likely that it was this family matter which netted him for K3.

"Am I right in suspecting that the rumour of payments leading to results at the College of which Ranek is administrator is what qualified him for K3 membership?"

The nods had indicated that this assumption was probably correct. Such a College would clearly have its uses for an organisation such as K3. There was, however, something more relevant the twins had been eager to tell Gina, whom they reminded had described Ranek as taciturn but also as if nervous that she might ask him something directly. In their view, this stemmed from the fact that he may have feared Gina might become suspicious of him because Ranek Malesh, the man with the qualifications, was his stepbrother! The Ranek with whom Gina had been acquainted was a Boran Myan, under arrest in Zanlandia for having assumed the identity and assets of his dead stepbrother. The real Ranek's money and property should have gone to his estranged wife and son, who in view of Boran's action, might take the opportunity to press for the strange circumstances in which the real Ranek died to be re-investigated.

"Please tell me there is no more bad news to be revealed about the Trustees? It is hard enough to digest what I have been told," The forlorn tone in Gina's voice had shown how much the information given had

119

shattered her. She had never liked any of the four. She had hated their defects of character and, in particular, their ineptitude as Trustees but she had never gone beyond that. They had been vouched for as respectable men. In no way would she have guessed their secrets. She had managed a smile as she remarked that Marcus had been truthful when excusing his constant unavailability whenever any contact had been sought, that he had been too busy!

The re-assurance from Simon that the Quartet had not been involved in any misdemeanour within the Charity had been pleasing to hear. Their interest in it lay only in the affirmation of standing and respectability it gave them just as Gina had identified from the beginning. Yet unfortunately, it had been their limited, casual interest in what being a Trustee meant which had accounted for the problems.

"They might not have actively participated in whatever crimes you are going to reveal but they definitely made it possible. It doesn't console me that I tried hard to establish 'due diligence through scrutiny and monitoring' but I failed, and that failure remains a bitter pill."

Chapter 27

Although the damning words had not yet been uttered, Gina had known instinctively that she was about to be told that some kind of despicable financial malpractice had been taking place. An article she had read had claimed that on average in the developed world, one in ten people steal from work. Thus, in an environment which presented ample opportunities and where stringent scrutiny was lacking, the temptation would have been too great to resist. It was inevitable that some would have had their 'fingers in the till' but it would have been foolish to hope there had been only some petty pilfering. Sadly, Gina had accepted that, some day, some serious embezzlement and chicanery would come to light and it seemed that day had dawned.

"Ready?" Maxim had inquired.

"As ready as I'm going to be," she had sighed in reply. "Let's hear the lamentable truth. What will distress me will be my lack of shock and disbelief about any dishonesty uncovered and my lack of expectation for the sums to be small."

What Gina had not expected to hear was that the investigations, which had taken over two years, had been instigated by Greg who had contacted Maxim shortly before his death. Knowing nothing about this, she had been eager to hear what had worried her Greg so much that he had taken action. In her heart though Gina could guess that he had been seeking to protect her, even from herself and her wilful reluctance to share her unease and suspicions with those she could trust. Her hesitancy had stemmed from her lack of incontrovertible proof. The greatest concern of the Quartet would have been to prove her wrong, not to listen, consider and probe.

The everyday opportunities for larceny would not have been picked up by the audit process carried out which never did more than note the money in and the money out.

"Greg had been trying to look after you," Maxim had confided, confirming what she had thought. "He wanted advice on the best way to obtain the elusive proof you wanted that would necessitate the Council of Charities to act. He was looking for an investigator capable of undertaking the task."

This information had touched a nerve. It had illustrated once again just how much her involvement with, and loyalty to, the Angelus and its good work had cost them. It would prey on her conscience that Greg had faced such a dilemma in the weeks before his death. The thought suddenly fuelled a need for retribution and the satisfaction of seeing all those responsible for her heartache to get what they deserved. However, this vengeful feeling quickly ebbed from a tsunami into a strong breaker when she remembered all the loyal, honest supporters and volunteers. As much as possible, they had to be protected from the worst of the fall-out a financial scandal would cause once the news became public. Then, her anger had surged again at the betrayal, pronouncing that she would be delighted if three particular individuals had been positively and unchallengeably identified as unprincipled thieves. This animus Gina believed justified as all three had shown themselves to be shameless liars, devoid of integrity.

Asked which of the three she wanted dealt with first meant that she had identified the correct felons, and so she had given the following order Rhyane Behn, Viana Weiss and lastly Rissa Lancie. Who was the man who had warned that neither Rhyane nor Ifan Behn, were trustworthy? It would appear that he was right. If Rhyane had been up to no good, then Ifan would have played a part. Several people had complained to Gina that he was using one donated vehicle as his own. Sarcastically she had commented to the others that being the self-styled 'Northern President', he would have considered this his due! Then there was the generous treating of friends to the tune of £3000. Suddenly, Gina's heart sank. How much had they syphoned away? Could the sum ever be calculated accurately? Such had been her thoughts before Pierre began to tell her the various ways used by Rhyane to line her own pockets: bogus and duplicated travelling expenses, duplication of invoices plus fake ones, taking and skimming cash from donations, cleverly lodging money in a 'pseudo' charity account in order to benefit personally for a period from the interest before transferring the sums into the legitimate account. To do all this, Gina well appreciated that some specialised knowledge and imaginative accounting methods had been necessary. Rhyane had been more active and cleverer than she had ever dreamt possible.

While she was thinking that the reality was becoming truly ugly, Pierre had startled Gina with a question: "Were you aware that Rhyane's assistant Linda was dismissed without notice but with a generous pay-off and a sum for her silence?"

Both the dismissal part and the fact that Linda had been warned not to talk had been relayed to Gina by a group of volunteers. They had written to the Chairman to say that it was Rhyane who should have been sacked.

"How right they were." Pascal had then told Gina that Linda had been dismissed because of a worrying discrepancy which she had queried to her cost. This and a lot of other interesting bits of information they had gleaned from Linda's husband who, as he had pointed out, was free from any gagging order. From what the husband had told them, the twins had been able to get a means of access to evidence they had wanted.

"You always need that piece of luck in any investigation and fortunately another came our way in the South with regard to Rissa's activities."

This statement by Simon whom Gina regarded as a 'by the book' individual, had made her reasonably confident all evidence had been acquired in a legal fashion. Nevertheless, she had sought to confirm this by asking:

"I take it that all proof of wrongdoing has been acquired without bending too many rules and it's rock-solid. NO, sorry, forget I asked, I should have known better."

Fortunately, all four had appreciated Gina's nervousness and fear, and had been glad to assure her there was no way the culprits would escape paying for their financial crimes. The work had been thorough and it would save the police a lot of time because the evidence which would be presented would be comprehensive. Suddenly, the thought of what it had cost had come into Gina's mind but a look from Maxim had made her think twice about mentioning the subject. The investigation had been undertaken as much for her as for the Angelus, her indebtedness to Maxim was great and it humbled her.

Chapter 28

To be told that Anya and her two part-time helpers in the other Northern Office had committed no offence had been good news. To have been informed the opposite would have been a real shock. In fact, Gina had admitted that it would have dented, beyond measure, her faith in her own judgement and intuition. However, to hear that Anya had not moved on, or rather that she had not been ousted by Rhyane and Rissa had been a surprise.

With regard to the office in Aswanes, once Rissa had ensconced her cronies, Gina had lost all confidence. The necessity to phone had filled her with dread because the response had never been a pleasant one, more 'yes what do you want?' The first time Gina met Viana Weiss, the senior of the four, she had become aware that this dumpy, pugnacious thirty-something had determined already to be her foe. From the facial lines, resulting from her permanent scowl, Gina had concluded that Viana was virtually at war with the world, well, all that is bar Rissa and the other three. Quite deliberately, she had emphasised her 'allegiance' to Rissa!

In view of this, Gina had felt confident in stating that whatever Viana had been up, Rissa would have been aware of the situation and given it her blessing. Similarly, in the case of Rhyane, she strongly suspected the same would be true. The two had struck up a friendship which saw them meeting up once a month for a 'girls' day out'. Several volunteers had complained to the Chairman having discovered Rissa's Hotel Bill was being charged to the Charity. The response received from the Office at Aswanes had informed that Rissa's monthly visits North concerned official business and their accusation had not been appreciated! The volunteers had referred the matter to Colin but, he too, had been deaf to their complaints.

"Ironically, they always said that Rhyane and Rissa were as thick as thieves. Furthermore, they had done their own checking and knew the truth but feared going public. In any case, the press had become too nervous to listen or to investigate for itself following the threat of an injunction. Sorry. I've interrupted. You were going to tell me about Viana's self-serving activity."

Through some quiet testing, it had been shown that Viana had a tendency to be light-fingered when dealing with cash but her main misdemeanour related to the 'in-house' quarterly raffle. Following very careful scrutiny and investigation what had been uncovered was that a great many prizes had gone to her relations or to herself using names and addresses provided by her brother who worked in an estate agent's. What made Viana's activity even more galling was that it did not appear any of these 'winning' tickets had been purchased, so her prize winners benefitted without contributing! The others hoped that Gina now appreciated why Viana's anger had verged upon unreasonable when she accidently stumbled into her 'Raffle Den'. The accusation of 'trespass' which had followed had been necessary to deter Gina from her 'snooping' by accident, or on purpose. As Gina had stated earlier, the 'over the top reaction' had made her suspicious, and very uneasy that she had to let the matter be.

By this time, the thought of how much money had been pilfered away by one means or another had begun to make her feel queasy. The small cash sums never officially noted would never be known except to those who pocketed the money. At least Rissa would not have had the opportunity for much petty larceny but Gina had not needed to be told that Mrs. Lancie had been guilty of theft on a grander scale by means of all the ways which had been listed for Rhyane and more as well. Immediately, Gina's mind raced to determine the what else? One possibility had become a strong contender but before she had time to share her guess Pascal had begun to speak:

"You'll recall saying how the appointment of those Executive Fund Raisers, especially so many, riled you greatly but…"

"How else could Rissa hide her ghost employees? It did sort of cross my mind at the time, only because I knew of a scandal about bogus supply teachers. Then, I actually chided myself for being thoroughly nasty and bitchy. Ironic, isn't it?" Though Gina's remark had sounded light-hearted, her heart had felt very leaden. She had said 'employees' before Pascal had confirmed there were two which over three and a half years had amounted to no mean sum. Words actually failed her, none had seemed adequate to fully express her contempt at the betrayal of trust. It had not helped the anguish Gina had felt to hear stated what was the blunt truth; it had been made easy for the three and it was more than likely they had laughed all the way to the bank.

Maxim had looked at her hard and had seemed to have read her thoughts because he told her not to condemn herself:

"You observed, you noted, you battled, you saw the red warning lights. If you had not been there, no one else would be interested enough to see, to question. Without you there, I would not have been prompted to take action and, by the way, Greg gave me copies of all your dossier of papers." His words had eased her self-flagellation and after all she had tried but no one had been prepared to listen: "Really, remember we're all good chaps here."

Chapter 29

Her spirits lifted, Gina had asked what names Rissa had used for her two ghosts, her alter egos. Whether the term was correct, or not, the others had understood. Without hesitation, Pierre had answered, stating Caryl Lane and Lena Larcy, both of whom supposedly lived at addresses twenty miles either side of Strwyth. Gina's observation that the names were anagrams of each other had caught the others by surprise and they had seemed uninterested because there was no relevance attached. Pierre, however, had been keen to know why Gina had asked for the names which he had been positive had not been from idle curiosity. Believing also that names she had heard had disappointed he wondered if another two, given them by Rissa's daughter when they tracked her down, might be those she hoped for, whatever they were. Furthermore, the names were those Rissa used for accounts in which she lodged her ill-gotten gains. Whether the hesitation which followed had been for effect or to tease, Gina had found it annoying, not amusing. If a drum roll had been wanted, then her heart had been beating loud enough to become one as she waited and prayed for the names to be significant.

"They are Nerissa Vasca and Neri Samuel."

Never before had Gina experienced such euphoric delight at the sound of four words which made two names.

"Oh, praise be! I truly believe we got her." The faces which stared at her had held expressions which ranged from startled, puzzled, to concerned. Simon had hurried to assure Gina that Rissa would not escape imprisonment for embezzlement.

"What I'm on about is incitement to grievous bodily harm, or even manslaughter if Tony Rohm's injuries hastened his death. The use of the name 'Vasca' is too much of a coincidence to be a random choice. Remember that surname I mentioned when giving details of the investigation."

Gina had so wanted everyone to share her excitement and hope but then she remembered that she had not told them what Don had told her just the previous evening. While listening to him an inner voice had told her to pay heed and that niggling instinct had been right. Her excitement had waned, however, as she relayed the details of Don's story and then recapped on the mention made of Nancy Vasca, even though her listeners had agreed the new information was relevant and could lead to a significant breakthrough. Nevertheless, although it had put that intuitive feeling of knowing on a much firmer and factual foundation, there was the matter of proving beyond reasonable doubt. There was the matter of those alibis, and the need to get proof that Nancy Vasca was Rissa's aunt, or a relation anyway.

Having digressed, and with time passing, the group needed to press on and discuss the most important matter of the day, namely their strategy of action in bringing the miscreants to justice. From the discussion which had followed, Gina had discovered very quickly that a lot of preparatory work had been done already. Maxim had been in contact with the Head of Cymran's National Fraud Unit whom, as he had emphasised, he trusted implicitly.

"Once the word 'go' has been ordered, it will be a slick, professional, co-ordinated sortie on all targets," This Gina had not doubted but it was good to get the assurance because she had begun to feel nervous, there was so much at stake. There had to be no chance of evidence being destroyed, and, of course, somehow the Angelus had to survive. Again it seemed as if Maxim had read her thoughts because he had told her that most of the next week they would have to be down in Fridcar. Anything on the agenda would have to be cancelled which she would have been more than happy to do except that luckily there was no need.

A meeting with the Chief Officer of the Council of Charities had been arranged for the Monday and Simon had reminded Gina that both the Chief Officer and his Deputy were new incumbents in the job. There was a need to ensure the Council of Charities had the power to take temporary control of the Angelus until new Officers and Trustees could be appointed. This presented a major problem; the Legislative Assembly's law-making process would take too long, the other alternative would be to get sufficient members to petition the President to use his power to introduce the needed law. Since the Republic's establishment this special power had been used only once. It had seemed to Gina that they had an impossible mountain to climb but the twins, noticing her downcast expression, urged her to have faith.

In a way, the Legislative Assembly members deserved to be left with 'egg on their face' for not listening and responding to the known need to strengthen the powers of the Council of Charities so it could police and act as a proper watchdog. The only reason they would be lobbying for action was their wish to ensure the continuance of the Angelus yet, come what may, the others had informed her they expected the arrests of the three embezzlers to take place before the end of the forthcoming week. This reminded Gina of the miscreant Trustees; Ranek was under arrest in Zanlandia already but what of the others?

In reply to her query, Gina had been told that Marcus and his brother had been lured to Manlah where the headquarters of the firm they worked for was based and so their arrests would take place in Zanlandia. The trading company set up by Marcus and the others had a distribution and storage depot in Manlah. Moreover, his wife there managed the distribution while his Cymran wife managed the production side in Aswanes and they, too, would be arrested along with Felix and Damon. Gina had wondered somewhat forlornly if she was clutching at very fragile straws in hoping that the Cymran media, in reporting on the arrests, would not note their association with the Angelus.

Then, suddenly through thinking about the media, an idea had boosted her spirits especially when it was supported as well worth a try. Her suggestion had been to try and get the Reporter of the article on Charities to write a follow up to be featured immediately, and that it might hint that urgent action to ensure better regulation was afoot.

"The reporter was John Haan," Simon had reminded, looking at the article. "Do you know him, Gina?"

"Do you?" she had countered "I've met him on a couple of occasions and he is approachable. His brother, based here in the North, I know better. He knows a good deal of the story already and certain individuals have been of interest to him! Alright, if I contact him and go from there?"

All had nodded and Maxim had deemed it a suitable point at which to bring the meeting to a close. There had been general disbelief that it was approaching six o'clock. The twins had to depart quickly needing to get to Tralyn where they were booked to stay the night having business there the next day. Simon had further matters to discuss with Maxim, who had told Gina that Jane and Nico, not only expected her for dinner but to stay overnight. It had been a long hard day and she had decided she would not argue, having company would be good.

As she was leaving, Simon had thought he should mention that when the bad news became public, some would wonder how the truth had come to light? They would speculate about a 'whistle blower' and if so her name might possibly be put in the frame.

Chapter 30

Before making her way across to Jane and Nico's place Gina had sat on one of the benches on the front balcony of Villa Cecilia to phone Ben Haan on her mobile. On hearing her name his greeting had been friendly and when she outlined her request as succinctly as possible, he had guessed that there was new evidence, possibly major! Although she had not confirmed his supposition, she had been pleased to accept his offer to make copies of the documentation she had given him before they were both threatened. The conversation had ended with the promise he would phone back later in the evening after he contacted his brother.

By this time, Jane had walked over to meet her.

"Come and relax," she had urged, "you've had a long day and so soon after all your travelling. Don't worry that you've not brought an overnight bag, everything's organised."

Expecting the day to have been an exhausting one, certainly emotionally, Maxim had requested Jane to do some shopping for Gina's likely overnight stay. Thus, on the bed, besides toiletries and nightwear, there had been a lovely dress and matching cardigan into which after a shower she had changed. Jane's choice had been perfect, delighting her hostess who had exclaimed:

"Oh, Mr Maxim will be pleased. He's such a lovely, considerate man, though a lonely one. Like you are, I would say."

The cosy meal with the couple had provided the ideal antidote to the gloom and despair created by the day's revelations. The only brief reminder had been Ben Haan's return call. His brother John had been able to get a seat on the morning flight North and on the 5:30pm return so it had been agreed they would meet up at noon at Valeria's Airport Hotel. Even during the night, Gina had been able to set aside her worries and regrets which meant she had woken feeling well rested. In speaking to Maxim before leaving, she had learnt that they were to meet the Health Minister and others at his home at ten o'clock on Sunday morning and in view of this meeting, Maxim had persuaded Gina to return to Villa Cecilia the following day and stay the night so as to travel together to Fridcar on the Saturday.

After telling him of her own arrangement for the day, she had commented laughingly: "It is certainly going to be all go. I shall not know whether I'm coming or going."

"Don't rush. Take care." This caution by Maxim had been echoed by her overnight hosts who had seemed very pleased to hear that in a day she would be back to stay again.

Instead of driving directly to Valeria, Gina had decided suddenly that she had time to drive home to check on things. This detour, however, had meant that it had been almost noon when she arrived at Valeria's Airport Hotel, luckily finding a parking space quickly and easily. The two Haan brothers had seen her approaching and had stepped out to greet her. In no way would anyone have guessed they were related, let alone that they were brothers.

After introductions, Gina had been told the first priority was lunch, following which they would adjourn to a small committee room which had been booked to allow privacy to talk. At least, as her documentation had been read, the two were aware of her concerns which, unfortunately, but not totally unexpectedly, had allowed three members of staff to misuse their positions of trust. No due diligence of monitoring and scrutiny had taken place so the temptation to abuse charity donations for personal gain had become too great for them to resist.

"It would appear that there are no mean sums involved but it would never have come to this if the Council of Charities had possessed the powers to bite. It should be the regulator and policeman for Charities, keeping a constant vigil, making inspections," Gina's voice had reflected the frustration she had felt when she had made her appeals, in vain, for some measure of help and support.

"You don't have to convince me," John Haan had responded smiling. "What you want is a follow-up article which perhaps hints that the lobbying for action has been getting stronger and the voices calling for legislation have been getting louder. You want to try and ensure that enough members will be ready to petition for emergency powers for the Council of Charities."

Gina had nodded, a little embarrassed, at what she was asking. Indeed, John Haan had been quite justified in asking why she felt that things could not be allowed to take their course? Why indeed? Except to say that the fall-out from the scandal hopefully might be less if the Council of Charities could take control of the Angelus temporarily to avoid it having to be disbanded. Gina had stumbled in explaining herself. Then, Ben had saved her by stating that John's barrister training before he became a journalist had been affecting his line of questioning. More important, however, had been the assurance that neither of them wanted to undermine public confidence in charities in general but that their fellow journalists might not be so sympathetic. Gina herself had thought already of some unfavourable headlines the breaking story of the 'clutch of bad eggs' involved with the Angelus might evoke. Being realistic, she would not have blamed anyone for making the most of the scandal. Her thoughts had included some rather scathing comments, or criticisms about herself appearing, with her resignation as a Trustee called into question. John Haan had added his warning to the others received, that many would wonder who had tipped the investigations off, how? Why? Not everyone, he had stressed, favoured a snitch or grass, whether justified, or not, and amongst this group there could be a dangerous minority.

"Another Job's comforter, I was given similar warnings yesterday, but it is better to be prepared." Yet, the shiver she felt had not been caused by alarm but by an increasing feeling that a dose of something nasty was imminent. During her return drive home, her shivering had increased, also her sore throat, though it was her incessant sneezing which had concerned her most. "Not now," she had pleaded with herself knowing that usually she never did things by half, and there was the trip to Fridcar ahead!

No sooner than she had reached home, a fit of sneezing resulted in a nasty nose bleed which had led to a moment of self-pity wondering 'what next?' Nevertheless, before she had given up for the day, she had telephoned Maxim to tell of her meeting at Valeria.

Her voice had given away her poorly condition and his advice, like that of Don Hale later, had been for her to have a hot toddy and go to bed. Her phone call to Don had not been to seek further information but had been prompted by several messages left by him urging her to get in touch. Acknowledging that a visit that evening would not be appreciated, he had told her he would call on the patient in the morning.

Precisely at ten thirty the following morning, he had turned up as stated. Whilst he had appreciated that Gina was not a hundred percent fit, his main concern had been that she recovered by the Friday of the following week. Greatly pleased with himself, he had told Gina that he had managed to get two tickets for the Business Club Dinner previously mentioned. There had been an assumption that Gina would accompany him, especially as the ticket and evening were to be his treat. His rush then to give her his other news had saved her from making any comment about his invitation.

The news, Don had told her, would not only satisfy her curiosity but, he suspected, be of some more pressing use as well. Following this build-up, Gina had been all agog for him to start, deciding that if he supplied good news, she would offer him lunch of cold meats and salad. He had begun by informing Gina that on returning to the Nielson's after seeing her home, the expected advisory session on investment had not taken place and he had been greeted back by a quieter and pleasanter James Samuel. This had meant that his ride home with the couple had allowed for more general chit chat and a chance for Grace, to express herself. In fact, it had given her time to mention an interest which, in turn, had led to an invitation to coffee the next morning.

"You may well raise your eyebrows, and before you make any comment, let me tell you it resulted in Grace buying from me Volume *IX* of the rare leather bound edition of Gregorius' Plant Illustrations." It had been clear to Gina that the sale had delighted Don and she had assumed that the price paid had been pleasing in view of the fact that it allowed Grace to complete her set of which only ten of this special twelve volume edition had ever been produced. Volume *IX* had been Don's only copy.

In view of Don's undoubted profitable transaction, just to tease, Gina had returned to the subject of the dinner, stating "Usually I stay the night at Kalmon Manor when attending functions there…"

"What you want to spend more? In any case, you won't be driving. Actually, I thought you would be wondering more about Neri and whether I gleaned more from the Samuels. My! Now I see I've caught your attention."

"Well, go on," Gina had urged impatiently. "I just hope you provide the pieces of the jigsaw that I want so desperately. Yes, I repeat, desperately."

Gina's impatience had been matched by Don's puzzlement. According to him, it had been a chance remark about daughters which had opened the subject. James and Grace had assumed he knew of Neri, their *adopted* daughter, both being very keen to stress that there was *no blood tie*, contrary to their own initial belief. The child had come into their lives through trickery undiscovered until Neri was sixteen. Very wistfully, according to Don, making him feel very sorry for her, Grace had admitted that a prank by a group of James' fellow graduates had cost them a great deal emotionally and financially.

When out celebrating their graduation, the pranksters had spiked James' drink because they considered him an abstemious, pompous prig especially in his loyalty to Grace, to whom he was engaged. Thus, they had arranged for him to awake from his drunken stupor in bed naked with a beautiful young girl named Myra. Unbeknown to all, some incriminating photographs had been concocted which led, when Myra not long afterwards declared she was pregnant, James and Grace to pay the money demanded with an abortion promised in return. They had paid to avoid scandal and Grace's father forbidding the marriage because he believed Grace at eighteen too young to marry and James at twenty-two had not yet proved his worthiness.

When they married soon afterwards and moved away on James' first assignment, they had believed all had been sorted. Then, four years later, a letter re-directed to them by Grace's parents had reopened the sorry affair. The writer, a Nancy Vasca had informed them that Myra, her sister, had died in a car accident and that the child she had not aborted, namely four-year-old Nerissa, had become their responsibility. Once again, fear of scandal, and of crossing the Vasca family, had persuaded them not to challenge, or check. What is more, Grace had admitted that when she saw Nerissa she had been delighted. She had wanted her, an unexpected miracle after being told, following the birth of her son, she could have no more children.

The joy, however, had soon turned to grief and disillusionment. Unashamedly, it would seem, Grace had declared their experience proved that nature surmounted nurture and very much so, once Nancy Vasca contacted her niece. The final hurt and insult had come just before Neri's departure for America. She had laughed about the way they had been duped and that the sizeable sum of money they had given her was a poor pay-off for having had to live with them. The 'ouch' which Gina had exclaimed huskily at hearing such nastiness had passed unheard, lost in expressions of sympathy from Don who had seemed taken aback by the depth of his sympathy for the couple whom, on first meeting, he had not liked.

With all the feeling her husky voice allowed, Gina had endorsed all Don's sentiments, likewise the courage of the Samuels in telling him the story uncensored.

"Nobody deserves a Nerissa, Neri, or Rissa, or whatever she chooses to call herself. There was no hope of nurture overcoming her nature!"

Then, Gina had congratulated Don on his success in getting her very significant pieces of information for which she had prayed so desperately. Not surprisingly, he had been keen for Gina to enlighten him and she had detected a hint of annoyance when she told him the long and complicated story would have to wait until another time. To placate, she had said that she believed he had helped by supplying a crucial link by means of which a probable case of manslaughter might be proved.

Once they had finished lunch, the news that he had to hasten on his way because she had to drive over to Zion, and that for several days she would be down in Fridcar, had not pleased him either.

"Are you fit enough to do all that?" he had inquired, clearly genuinely concerned. It was a question Gina had asked herself as well. Nevertheless, this had not stopped her reassuring Don that she had a week to get fit for the Dinner. 'Fingers crossed', she had muttered to herself as Don walked away.

Chapter 31

Due to her eagerness to be on her way before further delays, Gina had reneged on her promise to telephone Maxim before she began her drive over to Villa Cecilia. After Don's departure, Fay had visited which had been useful in that it had allowed Gina to tell her that she would be away for a few days. "Clearly some mystery's afoot," Fay had joked. "You never mentioned these plans the other evening. Whatever the reason, it must be important because you appear pretty poorly to me. Anyway rest assured, we'll keep an eye on the house and I'll tell Petra you're away but please don't try to do too much. Are you listening?"

Although Gina had nodded, while Fay was talking, she had been going through in her mind her checklist to ensure she had done everything she should before departing. These checks were so routinely carried out that they were done almost automatically. Greg had always said she fussed and worried too much about things, mostly quite unnecessarily. Yet it had been fussing and concern about the feelings of another over a matter of dress which had saved their lives, a haunting thought on which Gina had not wanted to dwell. Getting on her way was her main priority because it was already late afternoon.

When she arrived at her destination shortly before six o'clock, Maxim had been relieved to see her, having expected her earlier. He, like Jane and Nico, had been concerned about her state of health but she had re-assured them that taking paracetamols every four hours helped greatly: "Just wouldn't want to be too energetic, that's all." Still, the fact that Maxim had abandoned the idea of eating out and intended instead to send Nico out to get them a banquet for two from a recommended nearby Chinese Restaurant and Take Away, cheered her greatly, Later, when enjoying the feast, Maxim had confided that it was a lovely treat for him to have company for such a fun and informal evening.

The evening had been such a pleasant, relaxing one that neither had wanted to spoil it by any reminder of the business ahead. Only in saying 'good night' had she mentioned that Don Hale had filled in the blanks they wanted, the detail of which she would recount during their drive to Fridcar. At breakfast the next morning, Jane had been eager to inform her that Mr Maxim had been full of praise for the food, the *company* and the fun it had been.

"I don't know the details but I understand you have a difficult few days ahead. I do hope though that you do have some time to relax so as to have another fun evening… it would be good for both of you."

Gina's thoughts on the evening had been that it had eliminated that vestige of reserve and formality which had lingered between them over the years. The journey to Fridcar which had followed had endorsed the fact that they had become truly at ease and relaxed in each other's company. Except for some discussion on the information Don had given about Rissa's background and kinship to Nancy Vasca, which both believed would allow for the

144

attack on Tony Rohm to be re-investigated, the matters which were to occupy them in the days ahead had been ignored. In fact, Gina had decreed that they should be put to the back of their minds because the mention of people's greed and misdeeds would sully the beauty of the scenery to be seen along the two-hundred-mile route.

While mentioning Don Hale, Gina had referred to his strict instructions to be fit and well for the Dinner at Kalmon Manor for which he had paid for her ticket. Somehow, Maxim had known that it had been Don who had driven her home from the Airport. Consequently, he had queried if he was a suitor? "Oops," she had responded laughingly, "I clearly have to be careful not to get tongues wagging. Now, let's see, David Johannes waved to me in departing the Airport having travelled on the same flight. Then yesterday, I am back in Valeria and no doubt someone will have seen me in the company of the Haan brothers, and now I'm travelling with you. How many men does one woman want? Such a merry Widow! Although not so merry at the moment due to this dratted bug. But no, the friendship with Don Hale, such as it is, is purely platonic."

During the fit of sneezing, coughing, and spluttering which the conversation had induced, Gina had wondered how she could joke about anyone being interested. When the effect of the tablets wore off, she had just wanted to curl up somewhere out of sight being in no doubt that she looked terrible and that her choking cough was annoying. In consequence when Maxim suggested that they ate early and ordered room service to the suite, her flagging spirits when they arrived revived greatly. A change of atmosphere, she knew would have triggered off her sneezing and coughing which would not have been fair on other diners. Actually, sitting at the window of the suite's large sitting room with its view towards Fridcar below with its glimmering lights, had been quite therapeutic.

The next morning Simon had joined Maxim and Gina for breakfast before they made their way to meet the Health Minister, Troy Finn, at his home ten miles outside Fridcar. On approaching the house which was very modern and 'avant garde' in its architectural design, Gina had commented that it did seem there was 'money in politics', quickly afterwards adding the postscript that she was 'only jealous'. Her observation, however, had elicited no response because the door had opened, the housekeeper had been watching out for their arrival.

Pleasantly, politely, they had been led down a flight of stairs into a large room clearly intended to be a meeting room. Gathered in it were eight people, a number not expected and she suspected Maxim and Simon were equally as surprised. Anyway, the greetings had been friendly, but with people's names set out around the table, it had been clear that formality was expected.

Simon had mentioned that Troy Finn had a no nonsense manner, that he hated procrastination and, while maybe not generally liked, he was well respected. Theo Clark, The Minister for Public Affairs, had been described to her, sometime before, as an annoyingly indecisive individual, his hesitancy in taking resolute action ascribed to his wish for popularity. In the newspapers, he had been the subject of many cartoons because of his movement from Department to Department. Yet, despite his ineptitude, he always survived. Both Ministers had with them their Personal Assistants who appeared to Gina to be products of the same mould.

The other four whom Troy Finn had invited to be present were his wife, also an Assembly member representing the Progressive Party which was in Government, and one representative of each of the other parties with elected members. These parties were the Populist, Federalist and Green; the latter two parties held the balance of power in the Unicameral Chamber of sixty members. All three belonged to a growing band of individuals who, in recent months, had been clamouring for Charities to be better regulated. Additionally, they had advocated that a National Regulatory Body be established to review how well complaints, or expressed concerns, were dealt with by Public Establishments. Their presence had raised Gina's hopes of a positive outcome from the meeting.

Her optimism had been boosted further by Troy Finn's opening statement which said that all present gratefully acknowledged the courtesy Gina, Maxim and Simon had shown in seeking a meeting to forewarn of an unhappy and serious situation before it became front page news. The plaudits from the Health Minister, however, had not stopped Gina having to face several quite aggressive and searching questions based on her papers, criticisms and concerns about the Angelus. In different ways, Theo Clark had asked her at least three times why she had not resigned earlier in view of her worries about the lack of governance. Another question, which he had repeated, had been whether she had exhausted every avenue to bring about improvement? In return, she had countered by asking him to suggest what else she could have done? Outraged by her audacity in replying with a question, Theo Clark had exclaimed, "I'm not here to answer questions, you are!"

Neither Maxim nor Simon had been able to remain silent following this angrily spat out riposte. Each had pointed out how hard Gina had tried and her papers evidenced how her appeals for help and intervention had gone unheeded. The Council of Charities had lacked the powers to act and this had to be addressed. "Of course," had been muttered while the Green Party member's response had not been so muted.

"Damn it, come on," he had urged with a thump of the table. "Let's be honest, no man would have suffered the abuse Gina tolerated. Instead, following a few expletives, he would have walked out. It is known, and not only on this island, that when Chairmen, or Chief Executives, or both together look at Trustees, or Board Members, as their obedient minions, those who oppose the situation soon resign. They walk away and forget about all the things which had made them unhappy and uneasy."

This had given Simon the opportunity to move the discussion on by taking up the point about Gina's tenacity. "If Gina, Mrs Fiddes, had not remained and observed then no suspicion would have emerged and the gross crimes which have been uncovered would remain unchallenged to the continued benefit of the perpetrators. What is about to be revealed is not minor pilfering but grand larceny by three individuals."

Then, following Troy Finn's instruction not to mention names, an outline of the thieving activity which had been going on had been given. Only Theo Clark had expressed shock and a measure of disbelief – "How sure? No possible doubt? Really? ...How do you know? How did you obtain the evidence?" The others had accepted the truth of what had been disclosed without questioning but with sadness at the abuse of trust.

The next sentence uttered by Troy Finn. Gina had written down and underlined such was its importance:

"Let me remind everyone," he had said, very slowly and deliberately, "getting information by subterfuge is justified if it is in public interest. The misappropriation of funds donated by generous supporters is clearly a matter which concerns the public and certainly the larceny must be stopped, and every effort must be made to prevent it happening in the future. So what steps are necessary?"

Immediately, desperate to continue moving matters on, Gina had explained that the Council of Charities could not, within the scope of its powers, step in to appoint a temporary Chief Officer and pro-tem Trustees, or impose a new and very formal appointment procedure for Trustees and Main Officers. Its existing powers allowed the Council of Charities only to suspend Trustees, freeze bank accounts and appoint receivers to wind up the Charity. The consequence of doing this would be that the life saving service would have to stop and then a new Charity would have to be set up. The upheaval would undermine greatly people's trust and confidence in Charities in general of which Cymran had eighty.

No sooner than Gina had finished, all three members, who had been urging for new legislation showed that they appreciated the need to act. Thus, they had advocated a petition to El Presidente to seek a Presidential decree giving the Council of Charities the necessary emergency powers until adequate legislation could be passed. They had been in agreement also that this could be a quieter and subtler way to move things on apace, and speed was necessary. Only Theo Clark had expressed strong reservations about the proposal reminding everyone the power had been used only once and El Presidente had to consult with his four regional consuls. Furthermore, any Petition presented had to have at least thirty signatures from members of the Legislative Assembly. His main worry though was that his Department of Public Affairs might be blamed for not ensuring the Council had sufficient powers to properly regulate Charities.

It would have been wiser for Theo Clark to have said nothing on this point and just an exchange of glances between Gina, Maxim and Simon had shown that each considered a tactful retreat would be wise. Managing to butt in, Simon had thanked all for the hearing, which he hoped would prompt action towards a satisfactory way forward. Although Gina would have loved to have been a fly on the wall to hear the discussions which followed, far more powerful had been her relief to be leaving. Whilst well appreciating the necessity for the approach they had taken, she had to admit to impatience and frustration. At least, twice during the morning, she had wanted to say: "Hey, I'm the good guy here." Then, she had chided herself for being over emotional. The advice given by Theo Clark to her when leaving to be 'careful and vigilant' had not helped either. At least, Maxim and Simon had been positive that rapid action would follow if only to ensure any fall-out would be contained. Their discussion, however, had been cut short because the weather had made a rush to their cars essential.

Chapter 32

The weather when all three had entered the Minister's house had been heavy and sultry. On exiting, they had found that the possibility of a nasty thunderstorm had become a reality. A fierce roar of thunder, followed almost immediately by lightning had indicated the storm was close. In fact, when large droplets of rain began to fall, there had been no doubting it was overhead. It had been a matter of sprinting to the cars in order not to get drenched and they had only just made it before the heavens opened. Simon had mentioned his hurry to get home and when his car sped off, almost before Gina and Maxim had fastened their seatbelts, she had remarked:

"Wow, he said he was in a hurry and clearly he meant it." Then, when making the comment, she had realised that all she knew about Simon was that he was Maxim's solicitor.

Suddenly she had become curious to know a little more, but fortunately, Maxim had gone on to say:

"At the moment, all is not very rosy for Simon, his sixteen-year-old stepson is being troublesome, very nasty and resentful. Not only is he targeting Simon but his mother Zita as well. If she reprimands him, he does not view this as merited because of his behaviour. Instead, he claims she is acting on Simon's instructions and taking his side against her own flesh and blood. One appalling episode happened when I was visiting them a few weeks ago. The boy's aim seems to be to split them up, a step they might be forced into to save their sanity. Simon's trip North to me, I think gave him a welcomed and much needed change of environment."

Discussion about Simon and then about the deteriorating weather conditions, particularly the latter, had absorbed their attention during the drive back to the Hotel. Both Maxim and Gina had been glad that it had been a covered car park with a covered walkway into the building. As they were entering, the lights had flickered, and then flickered again which had made Gina, fearing the worse, rush into the Sandwich Bar Kiosk to buy a few items. Her foresight had been timely because as she emerged with her shopping and hot coffee, the lights had flickered a few more times before going out leaving only some emergency lighting and no lifts. One consolation had been that they had only five floors to climb, though it had seemed more than enough.

On reaching the door to the suite, Gina had felt a sudden panic, all quite unnecessary for the key card had worked. When they looked out of the sitting room's large window, they had been surprised by the worsening weather conditions outside. The circling thunderstorm had appeared to have moved on but in its wake the winds had increased to gale force with the rain bucketing as if from a cloudburst. In addition, day had become night. The forecasters had got it wrong, the hurricane had been predicted to pass well south of Cymran.

Luckily, the room had a candelabra with candles which they had lit to boost the one small emergency light while they ate their hurriedly bought sandwiches, downed with the coffee. Whilst eating, the subject of conversation had not been the morning's meeting but the lack of electricity and why the Hotel's emergency generators were not being fully utilised to provide the building with more than the emergency lighting. In view of the somewhat dark conditions, once they had finished eating, Gina had excused herself hoping a siesta might help her shake off the lingering bug. Under the covers, the storm and everything else might be forgotten for a while especially if she managed to sleep.

Noting the time to be two thirty, Gina had intended to be up again at four o'clock. Once her head hit the pillow, however, she had fallen into a deep, and clearly, much needed sleep. The time of six thirty on the clock when she woke had been a shock and a rush to freshen herself and get dressed had followed. Full of embarrassment at leaving Maxim for so long, she had entered the sitting room somewhat sheepishly at seven o'clock to find the said gentleman standing at the window looking out at the still raging storm.

"Is it seven hours a weather front takes to pass?" she had inquired as he turned towards her.

"Well, if that is correct, conditions should begin to improve in about an hour. Anyway, how do you feel? I think you more than needed that siesta and here's hoping it has helped towards your recovery."

Answering that her hopes were similar, and after apologising for her lengthy absence, Gina had hurried on to ask Maxim how he had spent his time in what remained semi-darkness. On saying which the lights had flickered and dimmed, the generator complaining at the demand on it, being the conclusion on which they had agreed. Then, as if by telepathy, they had rushed on to state: "Pate and baguettes!" laughing that they had been sharing the same thought. "Very far sighted of you Gina to have added the items to your rushed shopping. I doubt if other guests will be as well supplied."

With a glass of red wine, the pate and crusty bread, followed by fruit had been adequate and tasty. Not unexpectedly, there had been some reference to the morning's meeting but mainly they had talked about the people present. Gina had needed reassurance regarding Theo Clark's warning that no menace was intended. Maxim's belief was that it stemmed from the man's paranoia, seeing shadows where there were none. Even so, Maxim had been of the opinion that Gina should not ignore the advice completely.

This suggestion she could have done without and she had to bite her tongue from saying so. To stop her from dwelling on it she had rushed to change the subject to something lighter and more interesting. In fact, it triggered a whole flow of pleasant chat as they whiled away the time in the flickering gloom. Ironically, it was when they were saying 'goodnight' at around eleven o'clock that the lights burst into full power. With a measure of relief, Maxim had stated that it meant that the lifts would be working in the morning, a relief Gina had been happy to share.

When getting ready for bed, somewhat pessimistically, Gina had doubted she could afford the luxury of sweet dreams which Maxim had wished, not until arrests had taken place and prosecutions were proceeding, or perhaps not until after sentencing. After some initial brouhaha, she had consoled herself that some other news would divert attention. Actually though, neither her worries, nor her lengthy afternoon nap, had stopped her falling to sleep. Consequently, after another long spell of restful slumber, Gina had woken feeling distinctly better and even eager to meet the

Officers of the Council of Charities. There had been some new appointments in recent months and she hoped they would welcome the possibility of new powers and the means to make a difference.

Chapter 33

On driving out of the Hotel, it had been immediately obvious that the storm had left quite a bit of debris to be cleared and some structural damage to be repaired leading to the closure of several roads. The start of the meeting had been delayed an hour to eleven o'clock to allow Simon and others who were to be present to get into Fridcar, such had been the disruption to travel. Maxim and Gina had met up with Simon at the car park nearest to the venue they wanted, which had taken Gina aback because of its dowdy, somewhat neglected appearance. The building which housed the Council of Charities did not inspire confidence, it did not give the organisation a significant status.

Inside, too, the premises had indicated a need for repair and redecorating. Yet the member of staff who had greeted them was pleasant and friendly whilst also being businesslike and efficient in her manner. They had followed her up a flight of stairs into a fair-sized room where five people were gathered. The tallest of the five introduced himself as the Chief Executive, in post just over four months. After this he had introduced the others of whom two were Legal Officers, and two were Accountants. Except for one of the Accountants, the other three were also newly appointed during the last six months. This small team of five was supported by six other staff members. Not that Gina had given any thought to the organisation's numbers it was far smaller than the figure she might have offered as a guess.

The longest serving of the Officers who recalled Gina's name had rushed to explain their inability to be of help to her with regard to the issues she had raised. His haste to explain had riled Gina somewhat and had left her with a feeling that the previous officers had found their limited powers rather convenient. Rather unkindly, she had thought that with some imagination, or drive to push at boundaries, there may have been scope for them to do more. They could have followed up their visit to the Angelus, for instance, and insisted that they did meet all the Trustees. The knowledge of outside scrutiny might have effected a measure of caution.

Still that was the past, and Gina had gained an instant impression that the new Chief Executive of the Charity Council was a man who would want to establish an efficient regulatory body. Before the meeting, however, Gina had not appreciated that to exercise new powers the Council would need more qualified staff. Again in her thoughts, Gina had been jumping ahead before the purpose of their request for a meeting had been disclosed. On this occasion, it had been Simon who had detailed the situation which had been exposed which to a large degree had been able to thrive due to lack of governance. Without argument, all five Officers had acknowledged that bullying, bossy Chairmen, or Chief Executives, or both were the bane of Charities and the reason for the downfall of quite a few.

The detail of the wrongdoing which had been taking place, however, had been met with unbelievable shock with the Chief Executive exclaiming: "That's damnable! That really does explain the frantic action going on

157

behind the scenes as we speak. Troy Finn phoned me earlier to say the necessary signatures for the Petition to give us emergency powers, would be urgently sought during the day."

The thought of new powers and involvement in a 'juicy' case had enlivened the room with excitement and speculation. There was relief expressed as well in that the lead would be taken by the Fraud Squad from whom the Officers expected to learn a lot. In fact, discussion of the interesting period ahead had seemed to make the Officers forget the presence of Gina, Maxim, and Simon. When they had remembered their presence, there had been an eagerness to reassure that the Council would fulfil well whatever it was tasked to do and this would set a seal on its future work as a regulatory body.

When making their way back to the car park, Gina had admitted that she felt somewhat 'shell shocked'. In no way had she expected the meeting to have taken the form it did. It was Maxim who had remarked that trouble at the Angelus had shaken things up and hopefully would result in some permanent good. Before there had been any talk of a petition to 'El Presidente', Gina had telephoned Trevor Mason, former Chairman of EST as well as the Consul for the South West, because of their interest previously mentioned – to warn both that some unhappy news would soon become public concerning some Directors and Staff of the Angelus. She had done so out of courtesy but she had begun to wonder if this had been a gaffe. Thus, when she informed Maxim and Simon, she had been glad to be advised that her brief chat with the Consul would not affect anything.

On the drive back to the Hotel, Maxim had drawn Gina's attention to the newspaper placard which declared 'Lightning strikes Power Station'. Later they had read the full story, namely the lightning strike had caused a fire which, fanned by the wind, had taken two hours to bring under control. This incident had been the reason for the power failure and some areas of Fridcar and its environs were expected to suffer a blackout for at least another day or maybe more. Such was the damage that it would take many weeks before the plant would be fully operational.

There had been better news regarding the main power supply at the Hotel, and a guarantee that the generators would not fail again. Accepting this assurance, they had booked for dinner at the Hotel's Sequoia Restaurant. Soon after, a phone call had taken Maxim out again leaving Gina to spend the afternoon writing letters and answering inquiries by text and phone as to her wellbeing, and about the storm. The North had not been in its path.

When Maxim returned late afternoon, Gina had thought he seemed somewhat subdued. A telephone call from Troy Finn had given her no opportunity to comment especially as it had informed them that more than the necessary number of signatures had been obtained. Moreover, they had learnt from him that the Petition had been delivered because two factors had made haste imperative. From the Thursday, El Presidente was to be away from Cymran at an international conference, and his hoped-for approval of emergency powers for the Council of Charities had become more pressing. In Zanlandia, Marcus and his other wife, along with his brother had been arrested for fraud. Arrests had been made in Cymran as well, pertaining to the fraudulent basis on which much of the materials for Trygana Products had been obtained. Thus, Marcus' legitimate wife and daughter as well as Felix and Damon were in custody. Counting Ranek's previous arrest for false pretences, it meant the Chairperson and three Trustees of the Angelus were under arrest. The situation was such, therefore, that it demanded that action had to be taken forthwith to allow the Council, after suspending the remaining Trustees, to take interim control over the operation of the Charity. Indeed, they had been informed by the Minister that the temporary scheme outlined by Gina might well be adopted.

When the call ended, Maxim had remarked that it was good to know that things were moving in the right direction. She had not replied, mainly because she had felt so sad on reflecting that all was necessary because of a clutch of bad eggs. By the time they went down in the lift for dinner, Gina's good humour had been restored as had Maxim's, both also in agreement that they were hungry. At reception they had found a member of staff waiting for them, it had been deduced that no reply from the suite meant the occupants were on their way to dine and the caller had stressed the call to be important. While Maxim went to take the phone call, Gina had been actively trying to guess who it was who wanted to speak to them urgently. Her guess had not been Troy Finn in view of the fact he had spoken to them an hour earlier. The greater surprise, however, had been the reason for his second call: "We are summoned to meet El Presidente at eleven o' clock on Wednesday morning, an official car will collect us," after saying which Maxim had hurried to assure Gina that he was not joking. Then, while a stunned Gina had been digesting this news, he had added, "Say nothing! It's time to put all serious matters aside for now. Let's go and relax and enjoy the evening."

On being shown to their reserved table, Gina had realised that 'The Sequoia' was the Hotel's prestigious dining venue, a place where if you had to look at the prices, you could not afford to eat there. The large mirrors gave an illusion of largeness to the room, although Gina's guess had been that there was seating for a maximum of fifty. The grand piano was being played beautifully creating a perfect atmosphere in which to savour the experience of high dining and forget all woes.

There had been diners at four tables already making twelve covers in Restaurant jargon, with themselves increasing the number to fourteen in total for the evening. The music and the postage stamp dance floor had become too tempting eventually for two of the couples not to use. Secretly from when the first couple stepped on the floor. Gina had been jealous, thus, the words, 'shall we dance, Mrs Fiddes?' had been bliss to her ears. More pleasing had been that several more saunters across the floor had followed and it would have been hard to guess they had never partnered each other before. Since her return from holiday, due to circumstances, she and Maxim had attained a more comfortable and relaxed level of friendship than had existed before, when a formal reserve had remained.

Chapter 34

When travelling south, neither Maxim nor Gina had expected to be free of commitments on the Tuesday. In fact, if El Presidente had not summoned them to meet him on the Wednesday, their decision might have been to travel back having achieved as much as they could. Instead, with time on their hands, Maxim had inquired if there was something Gina would like to do, or somewhere she would like to visit? In the end it had been a suggestion put forward by the Concierge which had settled the issue. He had proposed a leisurely trip on the canal which would include lunch and, if interested in birds there would be quite a few to spot. The included pick up from the Hotel was at eleven thirty. This time had pleased Maxim because it had given him the opportunity to take Gina to somewhere he had surmised would answer perhaps a couple of her unasked questions.

"Intriguing," was all she had said and a fifteen-minute drive was all it had taken for her curiosity to be satisfied. Their destination had been a smart three-storeyed modern building, mostly of glass, called Valaton House which a sign announced to be the premises of Valaton Associate Services, Solicitors, Accountants, and Investigators.

"So you have brought me to where Simon and the twins work and what part of the Associates are you?" The directness of her inquiry had seemed to have taken Maxim aback which, in turn, had caused her to blush fearing it had sounded rude. Yet, without hesitation he had informed Gina that his company Valaton Ltd owned the building and he had a 40% share in V. Associates. The other 60% was shared between Simon, plus another from the legal department, the twins, and two of the Accountants.

Very quickly they had learnt that the firm had been commissioned to provide necessary expertise to help the Fraud Unit and the Council of Charities once all evidence had been seized. Simon had stressed that the guidelines all parties had been given aimed to eliminate misunderstanding because all would be working under intense pressure. The twins had made it very evident they could not wait to be in action. Furthermore, they had been very pleased to tell Gina that Felix, on being arrested had behaved in typical fashion. It remained to be seen whether he and Damon would be allowed bail. Marcus's wife and daughter, however, had been retained in custody until the case came to court in the same way as Marcus and his brother had been in Zanlandia.

Although the four Trustees who were under arrest had committed no crime pertaining to the Charity, Gina recognized the fact that, by association depending on the publicity, the image of the Angelus would be tarnished, inevitably so, when the arrest of its Officers took place. Still, she was heartened that the judicial system in Cymran, and similarly in Zanlandia, was speedier than in Britain. Though the law in the island was based on British law, there were noticeable differences which she had not paid real heed to before.

Importantly, cases came to trial very much more quickly, usually within three months. To the liberal minded, the sentences were viewed as draconian, with no curtailment of sentence from the time stipulated. The island had three prisons, one for men in the North and another in the South. The women's prison was outside Tralyn while young offenders automatically spent three years undergoing a strict regime of military style discipline. Once aged 10, any youngster who killed was treated as an adult. Quite justifiably, it could be claimed that serious and violent crimes on the island were minimal and islanders were very proud of this. Certainly the Legislative Assembly boasted that cases were resolved without inflated legal fees, or time wasted, and few verdicts were overturned on appeal.

Prompted by something Simon had said, this had been Gina's trail of thought while Maxim had ensured he had spoken to every member of staff. His management style had shown itself to be paternalistic and Gina had discovered later the very generous extent of this. His interest in everyone had made her feel guilty in having to bring his attention to the time. As a result, they had reached the Hotel in time just to transfer from vehicle to vehicle.

Already gathered on the barge were three couples, all from Zanlandia who were to be very cheery companions on the trip, at the end of which, there had been unanimous agreement that the skill of the boat's owners – a married couple – as cooks and hosts had to be commended. The joy of it all had been that the meal had in no way been rushed and the sangria a pleasant accompaniment. Two of the men had been keen bird watchers and seemed to have eyesight as keen as the birds they spotted. The hosts also had plenty of tales to tell.

Such had been the enjoyment of all on board that it had been six thirty before the barge came back to its mooring berth. Thus, with the light having faded, their companions had been glad that they had decided to delay their return by ferry until the next day. Like the others, Gina had felt comfortably lazy and even Maxim had confessed it was good to be chauffeured back. Both had been pleased there were no messages for them so the relaxed mood continued whilst over coffee, with cheese and biscuits they mulled over the trip. One story told by their fellow travellers had stuck in Gina's memory mainly because it came almost too near the truth to be funny. It concerned an adolescent son asking his father "what is politics? How would you define it?" The fact that Gina had recalled the whole tale had amused and surprised Maxim, or Max, as he had been called by their day's companions.

Quite naturally, Gina had inquired if he had minded being called Max? It was then her turn to be surprised when he had told her his first name actually was Maximillian which his parents and brother had abbreviated to Illien. The name and its abbreviation had been a gesture to please both his grandmothers who had been born in Russia. Having been given this information, Gina had thought it only courteous for her to confide that she was Gina Lucinda, née Mores, her chosen names having no previous family links.

When at nine thirty, her tiredness could not be held at bay any longer, and before she fell asleep in the more than comfortable armchair, she had decided it was time to call it a day. Although the bug had passed, except for a lingering nasty cough, it had sapped her energy more than she had cared to admit. However, what she did admit to before going to her room was her joy that Felix had behaved badly when arrested. It proved her accounts of his antics had been no exaggeration and as she had explained she felt no sympathy with his mother whose wrath, she had speculated, would have been beyond words. Then she had moved to a lighter note:

"Thank you so much for a really great day and tomorrow may we hear that we have achieved our aim."

"I'm very confident." This positive response, Gina had considered to be a good one on which to end the day.

Chapter 35

The car from the President's office had arrived to collect Maxim and Gina precisely at the stated time, with Simon in the vehicle already. The arrival of the car with its crest and chauffeur had caused a stir of excitement amongst the young, front of house staff. From their reaction, and the fact that the Hotel was relatively new, it could be presumed that this may have been the first 'VIP' occasion, well in their minds anyway. "Like you say, Gina, this has made their day, and I think ours will be made as well." Simon had sounded very confident. If the unexpected happened, it had been clear to Gina that she would not be the only person devastated, but this would be no consolation.

The Palacio del Presidente had been the residence of the Governor before independence. Not a large mansion but with a façade of white marble, it did gleam and look special. In addition, as the approach to it was via a steep incline, the place exuded its importance in a very dignified way as the car neared. Its main gate was guarded by two sentries shielded within their box. The central entrance was opened only on ceremonial occasions and so their entry had been through the gate on the right, that on the left being used for exiting. Again, at the steps leading to the main door, there were two sentries, standing within the usual style of box. At the door an official had been waiting to guide them through the security checks.

After this, they had been led to a small anteroom where there were coffee and biscuits. However, no sooner had they entered than Gina had been summoned to follow another official in order to meet the President who wished a private conversation. Suddenly, she had felt a little nervous, a feeling which annoyed her. The President, after all, was just an individual elected to office having served as Regional Consul. The former, namely the President, held office for six years and could stand for a second term but no more. The Regional Consuls were elected for five years and they, too, could stand for a second term. 'El Presidente', Konrad Nage had been in office for only a year and so could be unsure about exercising a power used only once before.

Instantly on entering a room, the walls of which were lined with books and in which the only furnishings had been a massive desk and chair, a large globe and two high backed, leather armchairs, Gina had felt the vibes to be positive. These had been endorsed in the way she had been greeted. The handshake had been firm and she had been startled to hear, "Mrs Fiddes, it is my genuine pleasure to meet you." Being invited to take one of the armchairs, she had responded that she had never imagined herself in a one to one conversation with Cymran's Head of State. The reason for this, she was told, was to inform her that he and the Consuls had been in unanimous agreement the request made by the Petition needed to be granted. Telling her first provided him with an opportunity to thank her for her perseverance, and through friends obtaining the evidence which had forced Assembly members to react and do what they should have done long before, in view of many other instances of the abuse of trust, less serious perhaps in financial terms but still unacceptable breaches. Actually, it had amazed Gina how much he did know. The way her enemies had attacked her with lies immediately following her husband's sudden death appalled him. He admitted also that the fact a Solicitor had sanctioned clearly ridiculous accusations, of which proof existed of their falsehood, angered him even more. Fear and jealousy, he had confided, made people stoop pretty low and he had advised Gina to heed his words that the praise for her ability, honesty, and tenacity, which he had heard, had been in superlatives.

Before leaving, she had taken the opportunity to state that without Maxim's generosity, the Angelus would not have been established and the evidence of financial abuse could not have been unearthed without his sponsorship of the investigations. Noting what she had said, Konrad Nage before ending the audience had given Gina an envelope in which there was a number to ring in an emergency which would make it a priority.

"In a search for a whistle blower, you may be cited as a possible instigator and not everyone will applaud. Regardless of justification you will have annoyed K3, brought scandal to the door of the Vasca family, who are not overly fond of scrutiny, or attention. Need I go on? So, in case of harassment, or if you feel threatened, phone that number. This is not to scare you but just to be ready."

The official who had been summoned to guide her back did not take her into the anteroom but into a Court-like chamber where those who had been summoned to attend were seated already. Taking her place where indicated by the name plate, she had whispered to Simon, next to whom she sat, "I didn't get any coffee."

Then, she had scanned the crescent shaped row to note those present, namely the First Minister, the Ministers of Health and Public Affairs, Head of the Fraud Unit, Chief Executive of the Council of Charities, Maxim, Simon and herself. Whether there had been some chat before she had entered, she had no way of knowing, but since she had come in there had been a hushed reverence of expectation.

When the main door opened, everyone had stood up, and an usher who had stepped into the room announced the four Regional Consuls who took their places either side of the Presidential chair. The usher, having moved to stand at the door behind the said chair, then announced 'His Excellency. El Presidente of the Republic of Cymran, the Honourable Konrad Nage'. Bowing his head to acknowledge the assembled group, El Presidente had taken his place allowing everyone else to sit. The usher, who had moved again, then began his chant of the very set words giving the reasons for the gathering and why the extraordinary power of Presidential Decree had been given to the Office holder to meet the need for emergency legislation in urgent, or difficult circumstances.

The preamble over, El Presidente had announced that by the powers vested in the office, and with the unanimous agreement of his Consuls, significant new powers would be granted to the Council of Charities as from midnight. This would enable the Council to step in to resolve an immediate problem. There would be further consultation with all relevant parties to extend the Council's powers further, to make it a very necessary and significant regulatory body working to prevent abuses and mismanagement long known but never addressed. In concluding, Konrad Nage had stated that it had been both his, and his Consuls', pleasure to bring about such an important and positive change. His decision when relayed to the Legislative Assembly was to be under embargo until all arrests had been made in respect of the situation which had necessitated his decree. A similar restriction had to apply to the Press and Media as well.

Once 'El Presidente' had finished, the usher had announced that The First Minister had permission to speak. After thanking the President and his Consuls for their appreciation of the situation, he had stated that the necessary arrests would happen at six o'clock in the morning the very next day. All search warrants for premises and homes would be checked very carefully to ensure there could be no challenges. Co-operation between all involved would be essential. It had been agreed that he and the other two Ministers present would be kept routinely informed of progress. To show the Council of Charities' new importance, the approved press releases would be issued by its Chief Executive.

Once all this had been said, the usher had stepped forward to ask all to rise for the departure of the President and his Consuls, this time by the same door. When all had left, he had announced that those present were invited to participate in a buffet but all officials were expected to reassemble at one thirty to review the plan of action at which Simon was also to be present. Last to leave the Chamber, Gina had been greeted by the official seen earlier who had informed Gina that the First Lady hoped she would join her for lunch.

Two surprises, what would be the third, she had wondered as she dutifully followed him to a lovely room where her hostess awaited. When the door closed, the First Lady, a petite, vibrant woman in her late forties, had indicated a seat at a round table. "You're Gina and I'm Janine and we're just two ladies who lunch. Also there is no rush, your companions will be looked after." The mischievous glint in her eyes had made her more attractive and definitely a person whose company Gina had known she would enjoy.

The lunch of salmon and salad followed by fruit downed with a glass of white wine had been as enjoyable as the conversation. Janine had herself experienced the difficulty of seeking to discuss issues with men determined not to listen. On leaving University, a senior colleague had made her life at work a misery. Firstly, he had not wanted her appointed, being better qualified than himself. Praise for her work had served only to nurture his jealousy. Disheartened she had left and having married Konrad, she had settled to be a housewife involved in 'good works' and helping her husband's political ambitions. In some organisations with which she had been associated, the governance, at best had been very weak if not poor. One body had found itself with debts, on loans it had not incurred, which amounted to £50,000, a sum with which the Manager had disappeared to enjoy.

Not once during the hour had Gina felt a moment of unease in Janine's company and when the official was summoned to guide Gina back, he was asked to bring Mr Xavier in for a brief moment. While the man went off to fulfil his task the First Lady had confessed to being curious to meet Gina's gallant knight. In fact, she had admitted this to Maxim whom she had tasked to continue to protect Gina. When they exited, the Official had been waiting to guide them to an awaiting car. Except to say, when being driven back to the Hotel that it had been a remarkable few hours, with which Maxim had agreed,

Gina had sat quietly recalling everything to reassure herself it had been real.

Once in the foyer, Maxim had asked her where she wanted to dine.

"Please, may we eat in the suite, the view of the lights is great, and I know what I want…" she had responded with an impish smile, reeling out her choice of menu. Suddenly, a feeling of elation, of high spirits had begun to bubble up inside her. Without comment, Maxim had gone to the desk while Gina had walked slowly towards the lifts finding it hard not to sway and dance to the soft music being played.

Smiling broadly as he caught up with Gina just as the lift door opened, Maxim had told her that he trusted dinner at seven o' clock suited and it would be as she had ordered. Continuing in a light-hearted manner, he had teased that he had thought 'The Sequoia' might have been her choice so as to lure him into dancing again.

"With soft lights and sweet music and a floor to ourselves, be on your guard, Mr Xavier!"

Not wishing to embarrass him further, Gina had rushed to say that over a cup of tea, he could tell her of the part she had missed during her special 'audiences.' In comparison to herself, however, Maxim had little that was special to recount and, on hearing her account, he had been of the opinion that she had been especially, but not undeservedly, privileged. One thing she had omitted to mention had been the envelope with its emergency number but, some five minutes later, she had remedied this and handed the envelope to Maxim. Immediately, he had noted the number and in handing it back had told her to keep it at hand, just in case. The last three words had made her feel uncomfortable, wondering what people expected. Personally, her view had been that there was over-reaction!

Looking at her watch, Gina had excused herself having managed to get an appointment at the Hotel's Hairdressing Salon, important in case circumstances offered no further opportunity before Friday and the Dinner at Kalmon Manor. The hairdresser had been excited that it was *Mrs Fiddes* and not wanting to be churlish, Gina had said she had been privileged to have been invited to a private lunch with the First Lady. The young woman was in ecstasy that she had been told what none of the other staff knew! "And Mr. Xavier?" she had queried nervously. "Nothing as exciting, just some official business," an answer which had disappointed.

The Suite's emptiness when she returned had been somewhat of anti-climax. Gina had been all agog to tell how much stir and speculation their morning departure had caused. About twenty minutes later, she had heard Maxim returning and not seeing her he had called her name. When she opened her bedroom door and saw they were both in the Hotel's towelling robes, Gina had laughed in saying 'snap'. She had been in the middle of changing while Maxim had been for a massage hoping to ease a stiffness in his left shoulder. The masseur had been equally as curious about the morning and Maxim had replied with almost the same detail, except that he had been viewing the art in Palacio's Long Gallery.

An hour later when she entered the sitting room again, Maxim, dressed in smart casuals, had been seated waiting. Gina had taken the opportunity to wear the dress and cardigan chosen by Jane but not seen by the man who paid for it.

"I'm honoured once more to have such a smart, beautiful dining companion," he had said, rising to greet her.

"Why thank you, kind sir, for such lovely words, my head's swirling." This had been followed by a curtsy and a twirl before she explained she owed the outfit to his generosity. In joking mode, Gina had gone on to state: "Enjoying your hospitality for almost a week, dressed by you, ouch, am I kept a woman?"

"Then you must be obedient and come and sit beside me so we can drink to your success in bringing about positive change."

"It's more due to you than it is me. I told the First Lady, Janine, that I thought you deserved to be awarded the 'Order of State'. Oh how Marcus yearned to be so honoured. Well, no way that will happen now." The latter comment, Gina had expressed with undisguised relish even though she recognised that to gloat over someone's downfall was most unbecoming.

A knock at the door had announced the arrival of the food trolley, the table had been set for them earlier. The food could not have been better and the clear night allowed the lights of the city of Fridcar in the distance to twinkle magically. The wine, no mean vintage and well-chosen to accompany the meal, had been a gift, courtesy of the management.

"What it is to be a VIP!" Gina had remarked, later admitting: "I feel I'm in a bubble which will soon burst and I shall be back to reality. In the meantime, I shall savour every moment." What she had uttered brought a smile in that it reminded her of what Petra had said, roughly a week previously. 'Tut, almost plagiarism', she had chastised herself while Maxim had brought her back to the present by asking:

"Is Madame Gina, the day's VIP, allowed to leave that bubble to have a dance? The music is playing a nice, slow smoochy number." Regaining a measure of seriousness, Gina had said she would love to accept but would apologise for her being such a bad influence because she had never expected him to use a word like 'smoochy'. Equally as light-heartedly, Maxim had replied that it was good, therefore that they would be returning North in the morning.

The dance had ended the evening perfectly and the sudden mighty clash of thunder and a fearsome flash of lightning had indicated to Gina that it was a good idea to wish goodnight and heed her head and not her heart.

Chapter 36

All sort of thoughts had kept Gina from getting much sleep and when it came to six o' clock, zero hour, she had given up trying. In going to bed the previous evening, none of those about to be arrested would have dreamt of a dawn awakening by the police armed with warrants. The shock would not have induced quiet submission; of that she had felt pretty sure. On the contrary, there would have been outrage and declarations of innocence. Gina would have loved to view the scenes from afar. If she had been asked to choose only one to witness, it would have to be the homestead of Rhyane and Ifan Behn.

Despite the airs and pomposity, more than once their behaviour and language had been reported as showing their upbringing. Numerous times, even after she had resigned, annoyed volunteers and supporters had accosted Gina to complain, with the following often repeated: "They're nobody, you know, and it does show." The embargo had meant there would be nothing in the day's newspaper about the arrests nor about the important change in the law. Yet, she had been assured that television networks would make some reference as the day progressed.

Soon after nine o'clock, just as they had been preparing to start their journey back, Maxim had received a phone call from Pascal to say that Rhyane and Ifan Behn were under lock and key in different Police Stations both vocal in their protestations. The next report had come from Pierre, his voice revealing excitement, the reason for which he had not given straight away. Instead, he had reported firstly about Rissa who after some initial screaming of abuse had then clammed up and her silence had remained. In Aswanes, on the other hand, Viana had been quite calm and very unexpectedly, on reaching the Police Station, had asked that her crime of organising the attack on Tony Rohm be included in the charges against her. Not unexpectedly, Gina and the others had been pleased that the matter, which they wanted re-investigated, had been so conveniently opened upon Viana's confession. Nevertheless, all had been extremely puzzled by her action, Gina especially, who had been adamant the 'admission 'would not have stemmed from fear, or fright'. Her speculation, which she had outlined to Maxim, had been that Viana was sending out some message to Rissa. If this was so then she had to have some evidence which, if she chose, could exonerate herself but truly implicate Rissa – a devious and dangerous game perhaps but one Viana considered would serve her purpose. 'Not convinced', had been Maxim's verdict on Gina's hypothesis. "You might find that, all along, you have believed the wrong person guilty of orchestrating the attack."

"We'll see," she had whispered, not wanting to create any discord, which was why she had hurried to introduce a totally unrelated subject.

Often during the journey, Maxim had been very quiet, concentrating on the road had been his explanation due to the heavy traffic making its way towards the site of a weekend Music Festival which they had overlooked.

With the journey becoming slower because of the hold-ups, and even the couple of detours which had been tried failing in their aim of gaining time, Maxim had urged Gina to reconsider driving on home from Villa Cecilia that evening. In her heart, she had wanted to accept but she had argued that it might be unwise to reveal any connection between them until the matters regarding the arrests had settled down. His sponsorship of the investigations should remain unknown and if some needed to point a finger at an instigator, a whistle-blower, then it was only right for her to become the suspect. To be accused of being over-dramatic had annoyed after more than three warnings to be careful and wary especially as her motive was to protect someone from possible harassment. The phrase 'better safe than sorry' worked both ways and Maxim had conceded that contact by telephone, or e-mail, might be best in the meantime.

On reaching the Villa Cecilia, greetings and goodbyes had been kept to a minimum, Maxim being concerned that Gina got home before the light began to fade, seeing that, despite the pleadings of Jane and Nico, she had remained determined to travel home. Once out of view and on her way, Gina had shed a few tears which she had considered merely a safety valve after a whole gamut of emotions experienced in a few days. She had consoled herself also that, once home and 'hatches battened', the need to busy herself if only to make something to eat would shake her out of doldrums. Her lows never lasted long.

Even as she entered the house, the telephone had been ringing. 'Welcome Home, Gina' she had muttered as she rushed to answer. The call had been from Fay checking that she was home. Immediately, on ending one call another had followed:

"What kept you?" a very unmistakeable husky voice had inquired part in jest and clearly from concern as well.

"Why hello to you too," she had answered. "It's only this minute that I entered the house. What? Don't tell me you're missing my cheery company already. It's only been an hour."

"In fact, I have," came the reply which made Gina regret uttering the kind of mischievous response which was often her habit.

After telling her to ensure everywhere was locked and to get herself settled in quickly, Maxim had signed off, informing Gina he would ring again around nine o'clock. True to his word, on the very dot, he had done so and Gina had been glad to chat, an antidote to the uncharacteristic edginess she had been feeling. Nothing had happened to make her feel spooked, but she had felt quite justified in being really irritated and annoyed because of the messages found on the answering machine.

"The cheek," were words she had stressed when telling Maxim of three messages which awaited her. The first had been from Colin wanting an explanation for his dismissal as a Trustee. The two which followed contained the same query and showed that Colin had passed on her telephone number to his remaining co-Trustees, the other four all being under arrest! Gina had considered contact by the latter two impertinence of the first order in view of the fact she had seen them only on two occasions and very briefly. At least, just being able to tell Maxim about her displeasure had been of great help, it had dissipated her outrage and had allowed her to sleep.

Chapter 37

On receiving her first phone call of the day at 7.45, Gina had concluded that it had been wise of her to rise and breakfast early. Unable to contain her pleasure at the news, Petra's first words when Gina answered the phone had been "Glory be, there is justice, or there soon will be when they're sentenced. Do tell me there's no doubt that they will be imprisoned for quite a few years. Personally, I'd throw away the key." There had been no pressure for information and Gina had offered none. The call from Fay had been along much the same lines ending with an inquiry as to whether Gina had spoken to Don. Next call was from the very man, very glad to know she was better. He, however, took it for granted that her stay in Fridcar had been in connection with the breaking news about the arrests and the new powers for the Council of Charities.

Gina had made no comment about his supposition, choosing instead to move the conversation onto establishing arrangements for the evening. Then, before ringing off, he had told her he had been a little suspicious of a vehicle parked near her house the previous day but, as a postscript, he added that she should not read anything into the observation; although, afterwards she had wondered briefly just what he had meant. A phone call from Colin, however, put any further thoughts on the matter out of her mind.

Colin's tone was more subdued than it had been in the message which he had left. The disbelief at his dismissal remained but then the news about all the arrests, it would seem, had passed him by, or he had not cared to believe what he was hearing. What he had seemed equally stunned about was that Gina had not warned him beforehand. "What makes you think I knew anything and I was not as much in the dark as you, or even more so. If you remember, my link with the Angelus ended a while back." Her anger increasing, she had gone on to say:

"And while you are remembering, please recall that you willingly, knowingly chose to ignore the blatant, ridiculous lies concocted to disparage me. You abandoned your integrity and chose the wrong side. Count yourself lucky that the limited liability clause will mean that you, and the other Trustees, will pay only a mere £1000 each for the lack of due diligence which allowed the abuses to thrive."

Gina's instruction to Colin that he waste no time in contacting his two co-Trustees to pass on what she had said seemed to have been ignored. Their phone calls had followed pretty quickly after Colin's. Neither could understand their liability for the £1000 charge because their presence at meetings had been infrequent! Not unexpectedly, Gina had not allowed this admission to pass, pointing out that governance and due diligence could not be carried out 'in abstentia'. This had led to protestations and excuses which Gina had considered to be feeble and cowardly. Suddenly these sycophantic members of Marcus' coterie could see his weakness as chairman very, very clearly!

Chapter 38

To quell her fury that all three men had forgotten their
unfeeling treatment of her immediately after Greg's
unexpected death, Gina had hastened out. Bumping into
two former hard working volunteers of the Angelus, with
whom she had coffee, restored her spirits. Both had not
disguised their delight that Rhyane and Rissa had been
arrested with Rhyane's husband included. The words
used in respect of all three were best not repeated. The
main grievances of the volunteers in general had been
Ifan Behn's use of a courtesy vehicle as his own and the
monthly, 'jolly' enjoyed by Rissa and Rhyane at the
expense of the Charity. Like Gina herself, none of the
aggrieved volunteers would have come close in guessing
the misdemeanours of which the two women were
guilty.

The companions with whom Gina had enjoyed
coffee refused to accept that she had played no part in
achieving reform and in uncovering the abuses. They
knew that she had resigned because things were not
right.

Chance meetings with other acquaintances all served
to help Gina think of other things and to delay her return
home. Not having time to tarry before getting herself
ready for the evening ahead proved a good thing, in that
it had not allowed her time to dwell on a message on her

answering machine. What it said had taken her aback more than a bit because, although the voice was muffled its sentiment had been more that clear.

"*Bitch.* You sanctimonious, interfering bitch. You had better watch out."

To have access to her telephone number so quickly, Gina had not hesitated in attributing the call to someone related to either Rhyane or Ifan Behn. Normally, she would have cautioned herself about jumping to conclusions but, in this instance, innocent until proven guilty did not come into her thoughts; however, her hope had been that once tempers cooled there would be no other threats. The need to hurry to get ready, had one advantage in that it had enabled Gina to forget the menacing message. Then, when Don arrived to collect her, his compliments on her appearance further helped to relax her for the evening ahead. That is, until a few miles into their journey to Kalmon Manor when she had started to suspect they were being followed. To have a motor-cyclist remain a distance behind them had seemed rather strange to her but with Don making no reference to their rear shadow, she had concluded she was being paranoid. Fortunately, the evening, in every respect, turned out to be the perfect antidote to any lingering concerns, real or imagined.

Sadly, the spell was broken just as they were leaving, all annoyingly through an innocent remark made by an acquaintance who had not appreciated Don was her escort and chauffeur home: "What, you're not staying overnight? Surely, you're not driving home?" the acquaintance had inquired. Still what really served to aggravate her qualms had been Don's annoyance as they approached the car. Not wanting the evening spoilt, Gina had hurried to stimulate conversation about the speaker and other guests. This had given Don a chance to air his views and opinions, an opportunity of which he had taken full advantage much to Gina's delight. As a result, the miles had been passing quickly and by halfway into their journey, she had decided that it would be nice to get home and not have to face the trip in the morning, thereby breaking into another day. In telling Don this, she had added that having company, and being driven made all the difference to travelling alone, compliments which clearly pleased.

Then, just as they had been approaching the most scenic, but twisty, downhill part of the route, Don had announced with some alarm, that a vehicle without lights was coming up behind them at speed.

"Some daft, drunken youngster, no doubt," he had pronounced. His next words, however had been overwhelmed by the noise of a crunch at the back of the car which had shunted it forward. During this frightening experience all each had managed to utter had been a jumble of words like 'Help, what the…'

Next, Don, who had kept his nerve and control of the car, in an unsteady and disbelieving voice had muttered:

"It's not that its brakes failed, for the vehicle's pulled back."

"Whatever you do don't stop!" Gina had instructed excitedly in response, wondering if Don was as churned up as herself, but there had been no time to ask because clearly aghast, he had exclaimed,

"Oh my god, it's pulled back to gain speed to…"

"Turn right, now! Now!"

These yelled orders by Gina, Don had executed without hesitation and quite expertly although the entrance to the dirt track road was partly hidden and tricky. Their escape to it had not been a second too soon, neither minding a bumpy, noisy ride if it meant escape. The track, which Gina had walked once for charity, after a short initial climb levelled out and then descended on to another main road. Gina's worry had been whether the car, with its damage, would make it, while Don's main concern had been how to get help fearing there might be no signal for mobiles. Eventually ringing the number she had been given, 3391191133, Gina had got a response, a very short and curt one 'give message' to which she had replied: "Gina Fiddes, help urgent, on track from A340 to A342, car shunted."

For what had seemed an age, silence had followed causing uncertainty that the message had been heard. Then when the phone had rung a voice stated: 'Rescue Helicopter despatched. Continue to A342. Repeat…"

Don had declared: "There is a God. Thank you, Thank you."

Very soon afterwards, a helicopter's searchlight had beamed down by the tall trees which made landing or rescue by rope ladder impossible. Its timing had been perfect to hearten Don and Gina despite the hike which lay ahead as the car decided to give up. With neither her attire, nor shoes, meant for a midnight trek, Gina had urged Don to stride ahead which he had done without argument. Only then had Gina turned her thoughts to the events which had led to their unhappy situation. Definitely no unfortunate accident had been her verdict, the car had been rammed deliberately, with the intention of causing injury, if not to kill, the stretch of road ahead of them being a treacherous one. At least, they had not been followed onto the track, but why was that, she had wondered? Had she heard a bang, a crash maybe? Was that wishful thinking?

Seeing one of the crew from the helicopter coming towards her had not been wishful thinking, or a mirage, and company for the last short stretch had been welcomed. More so, had been getting into the helicopter in which Don had been sitting already seemingly very subdued. During the short flight to Valeria, he had squeezed Gina's hand tight and once there he had been taken to see the Doctor at the base before being interviewed by the Police. It had not been a medical check-up Gina had wanted but a cup of tea which had appeared whilst she was being interviewed. Asked to recount every detail, Gina had started by mentioning the threatening telephone message, the motor-cyclist whom she had thought had been tailing the car to Kalmon Manor, before detailing all she could remember of what she called the 'ambush' and ramming. The vehicle, in her mind, had not been following them from the start of their return journey but that had been her impression, maybe Don had noticed it before his first mention of it. Anyway, in return, Gina had been told that the driver and his passenger in the offending vehicle were skilled joy-riders, and also petty criminals clever at evading justice though it had caught up with them, fatally, in this instance. Not the news Gina had wanted to hear.

Chapter 39

When formalities had been completed, Gina and Don were told they would be driven to their homes separately and the driver would remain with them until the Sunday morning. In view of the strain the ordeal had placed on Don, Gina had been pleased about this and he had voiced no objection. Nor had she, knowing that having company would be equally of help to her.

On arriving home, Gina had shown her driver/companion, Sonja, the guest bedroom and quickly the kitchen before retiring to bed into which she had climbed around 4:30am very glad to rest her weary head. The sleep which had followed had consisted of a few nasty dreams causing her to wake with a start on several occasions to the imagined echo of a bang. Sonja had been surprised Gina had not stayed in bed for the whole morning while Gina herself had thought eleven o'clock was late enough. After which the pair had spent a quiet day, talking mostly, although Sonja had gone through some personal safety measures with Gina whilst she had considered the property better protected than most against intruders.

Gina had been unsure whether, or not, to tell Maxim about the late evening events. Her dilemma was resolved by his phone call when she had found it good to tell someone how scared and frightened she had been during

189

the spell walking on her own, a spell which had given her time to ponder over the danger they had faced, and what if? Not unexpectedly, he had wanted to drive over but she had begged him not to and reluctantly he had acceded to her plea. What had happened on the drive back from the Hotel had shown that even her friends were not safe. She had not needed to be told that the car had been targeted which, after receiving a phone call, Sonja had confirmed.

According to what Sonja stated, the driving skills of the two lads were such that they had always managed to avoid being caught in the act of joy-riding, conveniently afterwards being supplied with alibis, though never by their sister who was their guardian. All three had been brought up by their sickly grandmother until her death some four years previous from which time joy-riding had become a serious pastime for the two boys. In identifying the bodies of her fourteen and sixteen-year-old brothers, the sister had been adamant they had never been involved in ramming anyone before because usually the cars they stole were found undamaged after their ride.

In her statement to the Police, the sister had left her brothers, who had complained of feeling fluey, watching a video while she went to have a bath and wash her hair. The doorbell had rung but by the time she got to the door, the boys were getting into a black transit van on the passenger side. She had shouted, to no avail. The van had driven off at speed as she approached it. On returning to the house, she had noted the time to be 21.10, and afterwards she had tried to phone her brothers' mobiles. The phones had rung but no one had replied. Her texts also had been ignored.

While Sonja had acknowledged the sister's statement to be helpful, unlike Gina she had expressed no sympathy with the young woman's tragic loss. In her mind, whoever had tasked the boys to ram Don's car – the number found the pocket of the youngest – had expected and definitely hoped that the two, like Gina and Don, would be victims of the tragic accident.

Sonja's speculation had gone further in that the spot had been well chosen which had shown good knowledge of the road. Moreover, making Don a victim as well would make it appear less suspicious and seem less likely that it had been arranged to target Gina. Although fairly similar thoughts had crossed her mind, to hear them expressed so bluntly had made Gina shiver. In fact, it had made her feel exceedingly cold because what had been said was not part of a novel, movie or nightmare, it was real – a reality she had never expected to happen and for which there was no justified reason.

When reports of the accident and the death of the two young lads appeared in the newspapers, there had been no mention of another vehicle. While Don, like Gina, had been glad about this, he had thought it somewhat unusual and had suggested Gina might know why. Her claim of ignorance had not been believed which had not been a surprise. Don was no fool. He had remained unpersuaded that she had played no part in getting more powers for the Council of Charities, nor any part in bringing about the arrests for embezzlement. Through all of this and other activity, he firmly believed that she had upset some powerful people and thus 'had become dangerous to know!'

"What can I say?" had been Gina's response, a little disappointed that Don had not offered any help, nor support if needed, in view of what he thought. He had not even advised her to be careful. Still, she had excused him, feeling he continued to be in shock.

After Sonja's departure, Gina had resolved to keep a low profile for a while and to be seen around as little as possible. Her resolve on this had strengthened when, just days later, she had learnt that Felix, on returning home on being granted bail, had struck his mother during an altercation causing her to fall and suffer a head injury from which she had died. Immediately, her heart sank feeling certain that her enemies would blame her for the circumstances which had prompted the row. They would not ponder over how Felix had restrained, for so long, from striking the old witch. Not unexpectedly, Gina's musings had been on questions such as 'why now?' and 'was she being overdramatic in thinking she was in a no win situation?' – The latter idea, growing after a visit to Tralyn.

Firstly, there had been a phone call from an Office of a Judge in Tralyn inquiring about Gina's availability to attend a special hearing which was being held due to the fact Viana Weiss was dying of cancer. The letter which had followed restating the details, confirming the arrangements made for overnight accommodation in view of the ten o'clock start, had eliminated any lingering fears of it all being a hoax. The mention of it to Sonja had led her to insist she would be the chauffeur and so just two and a half weeks after meeting, they had found themselves in each other's company once more travelling to Tralyn, the good thing being that they got on.

The next morning when entering the Court House building in Tralyn, Gina had felt inexplicably nervous not knowing what to expect. After registering her presence, she along with four other people, three men and one woman, had been ushered into a room furnished only with a large rectangular table around which were matching sturdy and heavy chairs. The middle-aged woman already in the room introduced herself as the Personal Assistant to the Judge who would be presiding, after which she had indicated the seating arrangements. Before any conversation could ensue, Viana had been wheeled in by a nurse accompanied by a prison guard. The latter had seemed unnecessary as Viana, her skin yellow in colour, was clearly a very sick individual. Indeed, Gina had needed to stifle a gasp, upon seeing her.

Regardless of her feelings about Viana, the person, Gina had been saddened by the pitiful sight and that she would die in gaol. It needed no expert to say that her illness was terminal. Yet, at the start of her statement, Viana had made it clear that she wanted no sympathy, she was resigned to her lot, a deserved punishment for straying from what was right. The way the words were spoken had shown to Gina that Viana's pugnaciousness had not been diminished by her ill health. Her statement afterwards went as follows:

"My parents worked very hard to improve the family's lowly circumstances. Devout Catholics, they would be appalled by my descent into bad ways. How did that happen? I fell under the influence of Rissa Lancie who seemed to care and be interested in me when no one else had been, except to bully. Then at the previous Charity where we met and worked, she contrived for a couple of financial prizes to come my way which I did not question. I was enmeshed in her activities."

"By the time I went to work for the Angelus Charity after Rissa's appointment, and then her rapid promotion,

I feared that my conscience had left me. If it whispered, it was placated by what Rissa repeated often, namely that it would be a sin not to take advantage of the opportunities the Board allowed through 'lack of governance and due diligence'. Rissa used to laugh at how easy it was to persuade Chairman Marcus of everyone's integrity being 'all good chaps' – or the female equivalent. I have tapes to prove this and my record-keeping activity is thorough. This morning, my solicitor delivered everything to the Court and my records will make interesting, but damning reading."

"Mrs Fiddes, Rissa hated you from day one because you could spoil her plans, you probed too much, and once Rhyane, who despised you for being respected, was appointed, the two plotted to get rid of you. I condoned it by saying nothing. It was only when I was diagnosed with terminal cancer, a month before my arrest, that my conscience slowly began to stir. Even so, when arrested, I tried to save Rissa from any charge with regard to Tony Rohm by stating that it was me who arranged for him to be attacked 'It's a far, far better thing' and all that. Although we, that is Rissa, Rhyane and myself, are in lock down at Tralyn Prison, all it needed was for me to hear that Rissa was concerned and inquiring about my health, and I would have carried through my 'noble' intention. Through her insensitivity to my situation, I awoke to the truth of how foolishly beguiled I have been. No pity, I was taught to know better."

Pausing to take some water, Viana had winced, clearly suffering from quite a twinge of pain but so that no comment was made, she had hurried to continue.

"The evening Tony Rohm was attacked, I rang Rissa at her home intending to explain that I needed to be off work another week. Her son had answered and he informed me that his mother had only just left to drive over to the Office. I cannot explain why but immediately on putting the phone down, I persuaded my brother to drive me to the Office in his van and I insisted that he had his expensive camera with him. When we arrived, Rissa's car was parked in the road and she was sitting in it. We parked on the opposite side at a spot which gave us a clear view of the entrance to the office car park. Rissa got out of her car and I noticed her red high heels. Next photograph my brother took some minutes later was of Rissa appearing again in the company of two men to whom she gave an envelope. After this, Rissa got into her car and drove home - time of arrival I got from her son who gave me the red shoes rescued from the bin. We waited hoping to follow the two whom I could not identify but they must have left the premises by climbing over the wall at the back, certainly not via the front because we stayed put for thirty minutes."

"I thought Rissa would frame Tony not have him beaten up. All this important evidence and photographs should have been handed over at the time, as well as Tony's travel rug. It is patterned on one side, plastic the other. Well, I have presumed it is Tony's. It arrived, in the post about a month after the incident. Who sent it I don't know but the packaging has been handed over."

The Barrister from the Prosecution Service, in questioning Viana about her statement, made no allowance for her condition when seeking clarity on some points and more detail on others. On three occasions, Viana's own barrister had asked for the question to be re-phrased. A query from the Judge about the significance of the red shoes had allowed Nancy Vasca to speak. She had stated that her niece, by wearing red shoes and an anklet, had been trying to incriminate her. Briefly she had explained Rissa's background and that at the time of Tony's attack, the two had quarrelled because her niece resented being criticised for her behaviour. The night of the incident she explained, she had been recovering from surgery to replace her hip, a fact not known by Rissa, also known as Neri and Nerissa.

"Mrs Fiddes," the abruptness of the Judge's tone had startled Gina, "have you any questions or any statement you wish to make?" Hurriedly she had gathered her thoughts into a statement that hopefully was brief and not trite.

"Your Honour, I am sure that I was invited to be present today because I was a founding Trustee of the Angelus Charity and I remained associated with the Charity until two years ago. I am very grateful to have been able to witness the courage and the honest recognition of her wrong-doing by Ms. Weiss and her wish for no sympathy regarding her plight. Regrettably, appointments were made without due process and the lack of diligence by the Board provided an environment that made the temptation to embezzle too great to resist."

"I am aware of how hard you tried to ensure good governance and how you sought help to improve things. Ms. Weiss has acknowledged this in her statement and how you were vilified for your efforts"

"Judge, my niece, Rissa Lancie, despised Mrs Fiddes for her efforts to monitor and scrutinise to ensure everything was done properly. I never suspected that her anger stemmed from the fact she was indulging in fraud, not from a Charity, and yet…"

Gina had never expected Nancy Vasca to speak up in this way and she had a feeling more might have been said if the Judge had not intervened with a 'Thank you'.

Taking advantage of a pause, Gina had blurted that she hoped the new evidence would enable the family of the late Tony Rohm to get closure. Both Viana and Nancy had seemed genuinely startled to learn of the young man's death. This had prompted Gina to add: "I believe his head injury at the time contributed because he died of cerebral haemorrhage." Following this, Viana had asked to be excused and she had been wheeled out. Then the Judge had dismissed Gina and Nancy, having first thanked them for attending. The others had been held back as he wanted to discuss with them various relevant matters and the new documentation received.

Chapter 40

During the drive back from Tralyn, Gina had given Sonja a brief summary of the morning. Both had acknowledged that, hopefully, the prosecution's task in *two* cases had been made easier by Viana's sworn evidence and her documentation, which, by her own admission was incriminating. Yet while Sonja had been able to state very dispassionately 'those who commit a crime should expect to face punishment when caught', Gina's feelings had not been so clear cut, being equally angry that the crimes should have happened at all. Their views expressed, the two women had turned to lighter topics which had resulted in quite a bit of mirth. This had not distracted Gina from quietly deciding that it was time for her to move from the island. Undoubtedly some might judge it as running away. In any case, it was not something that could happen quickly, there was the house to sell.

Ironically, when they arrived back, Sonja in approaching the property had commented: "Where you live is gorgeous, lovely views and the house is great. The kind of place that would have the buyers queuing up."

"Queuing up out of curiosity mostly," Gina had replied, cynically, laughingly adding, "if you know somebody who would offer the right price then saying 'yes' would not be hard."

"Seriously?"

Gina's response to the query with a shrug, had left Sonja even more uncertain but the doorbell had rung almost as soon as they had entered the house preventing her from pursuing the subject. The visitor was Petra very glad that, at last, she had caught up with Gina whom she declared to be very elusive since returning from holiday.

"You timed it right, you can join Sonja and myself and have some tea. By the way, you did not have to bring me a present," Gina had remarked with a grin, noticing the beautifully wrapped square box Petra had put on the kitchen table.

"It's not from me. *Don,* maybe or some other admirer? The card alas must be inside," Petra's hope of some gossip once Gina had opened the box being very evident. Instead a bewildered Petra had found herself facing quick fired questions from Gina regarding its delivery while Sonja quietly, carefully removed the box to place it outside on the back lawn. Afterwards she had phoned her boss, Seth Novak, requesting he hastened over. In order not to over-alarm Petra, who was no fool, Gina had told her that she merely feared the anonymous phone menace had gone further and resorted to some unfunny practical joke. The explanation, whether believed or not, had led Petra to move the conversation on to another topic while they sat and enjoyed their cup of tea and cake. When leaving, however Petra had reminded Gina that she was a true and dependable friend always ready to help. Afterwards, just with a hug, the two had got the reassurance each wanted which had been endorsed by Gina's thumbs up to her friend's shout of 'remember' as she drove off.

Even before Gina had closed the door, another car had arrived from which three men exited, one of whom she recognised, having met him at Valeria the night of the incident. What surprised Gina, more than their speedy arrival, was the fact that on Sonja's instruction, the group had brought with them a take-away selection for all to enjoy and while hot, the parcel could wait! The general opinion had been that if the intention had been to trigger it remotely then this would have been done within minutes of the delivery.

Funnily, Gina had not once imagined that the box actually might contain an explosive device. In her quiet speculation, she had been inclined towards some nasty dead creature like a rat. Her guess had been almost correct, the box, it was discovered, had contained a creature, very much alive and very deadly. Inside had been a scorpion, later identified as a 'parabuthus tranvaalicus', whose sting could cause the death of a human. Just where the two men sent with Seth Novak went with the box, Gina never inquired, being only too eager to have it out of the house.

From the beginning she had stated that she had believed the parcel had come from someone who did not know about the previous attempt to harm her. Questioned by Seth to explain her opinion, she had listed three reasons: it followed too closely the other incident; and those responsible for instigating it would expect her to still be nervous, suspicious, jumpy, especially when an unexpected parcel arrived, however beautifully it was packaged; lastly there had been no card. Of course one could have dropped off but Gina doubted this to be so and this had heightened her suspicion.

Neither Sonja, nor her boss Seth Novak, had tried to counter Gina's thinking, both agreeing that it was likely that there were two groups who wished her harm. To think it herself was one thing but hear it said aloud was another. All sort of emotions had stirred inside her, arising mainly from the fact that she had never dreamt of any such reaction, which was so undeserved. Though logic told her it was wrong to tar the whole populace with the actions of a few, Gina knew that for her the island had soured. The sooner she could leave the better and with emotion overwhelming she had blurted:

"Even one group wanting one dead is too many. I am truly spooked, so much so I wish I could pack up now and disappear. I came back from holiday with the thought of selling up and moving away from Cymran. Now my mind is made up but I can't run away and leave everything, more's the pity!"

Cutting across Sonja, Seth Novak had seemed both relieved and excited by Gina's declaration: "Are you genuinely serious about wanting to leave the island?"

"Very, and let's be honest, it would remove the problem of protecting me."

"Don't do it just for that reason. You're upset...." Sonya had seemed very unsettled by what Gina had said, and in mentioning her friends, Gina had so wanted to tell her that in leaving she hoped she would be protecting them. For instance, what would have happened if she allowed Petra to open her 'gift' as she wanted to do?

Noting that the time was nine o'clock Gina had urged Seth and Sonja to be on their way assuring them that she would be fine on her own. Reluctantly they had acceded to her wishes but she had known, without being told, that she would be seeing one or other of them, if not both, again soon. Relishing the peace and space of being on her own, she had looked up a half remembered quote from a poem by Byron which went as follows:

'The mind that broods o'er guilty woes
Is like the scorpion girt by fire
One sad, and sole relief she knows,
The sting she nourished for her foes'
(Giaour)

If she had hoped it would provide her with some
kind of answer, it had not, on the contrary it had left
Gina more bemused.

Chapter 41

The days following the scorpion incident had appeared particularly long even though Gina had found plenty to get on with in the house. The time had been punctuated with calls to check that she was alright but these had succeeded only in unsettling her. Despite her best efforts, the news that Viana had died, she had found hard to ignore. A comment Sonja had made that, by dying, the woman had escaped her punishment had seemed extremely callous. To be told not to waste sympathy on someone who had wronged her, had not helped, instead it had increased Gina's sadness at the way things were unfolding.

On the fifth day, Seth Novak had visited to present Gina with a proposal, the details of which were all laid out in an official document. No immediate answer had been expected, the advice given had been that she should discuss it all with her solicitor. Initially the contents had stunned her greatly but once she had assimilated what was being offered she had not hesitated in affirming her acceptance. Even so, there had been an insistence that she considered the matter for two days and, if her answer remained unchanged, the necessary arrangements would be in place two days after that.

Once Seth had left, Gina had wasted no time in getting on with what needed to be done, all of which led to many waves of differing emotions. The offer which had been presented had the Presidential seal and its aim was to try and ensure her safety. With regret, the State of Cymran acknowledged its limitations in this respect. Thus, in order to enable a quick departure from the island, the state was prepared to compensate Gina for the loss of property, earnings, inconvenience and so on. Furthermore, to enable Gina to have time to consider her future after leaving, the deal included accommodation for three months in the country of her choice to be arranged by its Embassy there. The hardest part of the agreement had been the commitment required of her, namely not to tell anyone of her departure, nor destination, nor to make any contact thereafter for twelve months. A change of name had been stipulated as well, all decreed necessary for her protection.

After this, trying to act as normal as possible had been difficulty. When speaking to her friends. Gina's fervent hope had been that she had managed to tell each of them in some natural way how much she had valued their friendship. The most difficult of the calls had been received from Maxim, to whom if she had been honest she had wanted to pour out her heart. It had been hard to listen to his update on the situation regarding the Angelus, which he foresaw being funded in future by the State as Sky Med, and that the case against Rissa and Rhyane were very watertight. Even more good to hear had been his report that progress was being made in the case of Tony Rohm whose family would get justice or, at least, so it was firmly hoped. Still, his news on the above had made it easier for Gina to reiterate her heartfelt thanks for all his help and how she had enjoyed the time in his company in Fridcar.

"I don't see why we can't meet up, if only for a meal?"

"Maxim, I would love to say 'yes' but, at the moment, I do seem rather 'dangerous to know'. Don't fret, all is in hand. Be patient and you'll get the whole story. Meanwhile, my love to Jane and Nico."

"Don't I get your love?" Maxim had inquired somewhat catching Gina off guard.

"You certainly do and lots of it, very sincerely so, as well as lots of thanks."

Above all, Gina had wanted to emphasise her thanks so that Maxim would never think she had departed without saying 'goodbye' because she was angry that the investigations he had sponsored had put her in danger.

On finishing her phone call with Maxim, in spite of her tears and feelings of yearning, Gina had concluded that her flight from Cymran was timely and to the good. In her heart she had felt a growing attraction to Maxim which realistically, she believed had no future and just stemmed from a great feeling of loneliness during a difficult time. The arrival of Sonja to spend the last day and hours with Gina before she left Cymran had saved her from a whole gamut of negative thoughts.

At Valeria Airport, the formalities had been dealt with by Seth Novak and he accompanied Gina and Sonja on the private plane for the flight to Manlah from where Gina had travelled on to her destination alone. Company awaited on her arrival, however, in the form of a young woman who had taken her to an apartment in a building where she also lived. This was convenient as the same young woman had been tasked to pick her up the following morning and take her to meet new people and to get her bearings. Much to the surprise of her hosts, within a week as a result of a good general conversation with a new acquaintance, their new guest had decided to go off on a twelve-week stint of Voluntary Service Overseas. Gina would have committed to a longer period except that she had wanted to be in the U.K. on a certain date.

Despite the heat, flies and conditions quite outside her comfort zone and not really conducive to her health, the experience of teaching children eager to learn had been rewarding. Deciding on a few days of recuperation in the country's modern capital before flying to the U.K. for her annual pilgrimage, Gina had found herself facing an unwanted, tricky situation, which did not make her feel good about herself. Signing in at the Hotel's Reception, she had turned and had found David Johannes standing there.

"My God," he exclaimed, "Mrs Gina Fiddes, a ghost walks!"

"Clearly I have a double, sir," she had managed to respond, glad to feel her colour drain rather than redden with embarrassment. The appearance of a young porter to deal with her luggage and accompany her to the room had been timely but Gina had known her escape to be only temporary.

Emerging from the lift to go to dinner, she had found David Johannes waiting for her having heard her book a table at the Restaurant when at the desk. His approach Gina had considered clever, being his guest at dinner would give him a means of apologising and allow him to tell her about the person for whom she had been mistaken, about whom she must be a bit curious. It worked because Gina had been intrigued to learn of any news from Cymran. She had not expected, however, to hear there had been a report issued that Mrs Gina Fiddes had died following injuries caused by a parcel bomb. Stopping herself from blurting out an anguished 'Oh, no!' had been hard. Her sad demise had led to the new legislation regarding Charities to be described as Fiddes Laws in her memory. The comments she had made, on being told all this, she had deemed afterwards to have been trite, though she had wondered how she had managed to make any comment considering the way she had been feeling at the time.

Anyway, David Johannes had continued, without hesitation, to give Gina the news he had thought relevant. Subtly, politely his choice of words had indicated that he still believed his dinner guest was Gina Fiddes. He had played the game and all she could hope was that he had recognised there were strong reasons for the subterfuge. All that mattered to Gina had been the tidings that Marcus was serving twelve years in prison with his respective wives having been sentenced to five years. Damon had been fined heavily for his connection to Marcus' business. Felix had been found not fit to plead in respect of the death of his mother but Boran (aka Ranek) had been found to be responsible for the death of his brother and had been given life imprisonment. Rissa had pleaded guilty to embezzlement and instigating an attack on Tony Rohm and in return her sentence had been reduced to sixteen years in total. Rhyane Behn likewise pleaded guilty gaining her a seven-year sentence, three years more than husband Ifan who had pleaded guilty to knowingly participating and helping his wife. Finally, Nancy Vasca had escaped being incarcerated, through helping to get Rissa to admit her actions, but she had been fined for perverting the course of justice in the first instance. From all that Gina had gleaned, it had been clear to her that David Johannes had followed each of the trials carefully.

"A bad bunch of people well dealt with" had been his conclusion nearly catching Gina out by remembering parts of John Haan's article and asking if she had read it. Then, following her reminder that he was talking to Gina Fiddes' double, he had remarked that having been assumed to be the whistle-blower, Gina Fiddes had made powerful enemies and had paid the price.

At the end of the meal and when she had been about to step into the lift in addition to saying 'goodnight', he had added with a mischievous glint in his eye;

"Tell me your name again." The doors had closed conveniently but not before she had heard him say "Your secret is safe."

A secret, such as hers, did present problems as she had found making her arrangements regarding the U.K. Better to keep to my new name, had been her conclusion. This had meant that she had to choose to stay somewhere different when visiting the cemetery where the ashes of Greg and daughter Gillian were interred. Actually her new choice of hostelry had pleased Gina greatly because its 'olde worldly' charm was warm and cosy, important to her as her pilgrimage, on this occasion, had more poignancy than ever. To her surprise, she had found a beautiful bouquet of fresh flowers at the gravestone where the ashes of both lay. The card had been pristine indicating the flowers had not been there long and on it, all that had been written was:

'From a caring friend'.

Somewhat disconcerted, Gina had turned around but no other person had been visible. On leaving, however she had seen at the end of the path, a figure that was no mirage. Nevertheless, she had pinched herself hard to prove to herself she was awake. How was it possible? Then she had remembered telling Maxim that at twelve noon on Gillian's birthday anniversary, she and Greg had established the ritual which she continued in memory of both.

"Lucinda Mores, I believe."

"You lovely, lovely, clever man! You guessed I would use my second name and maiden name."

His greeting had filled Gina Lucinda with such joy and an instant hope of an interesting and happy future ahead.

Alphabetical List of Named Characters

Rhyane Behn – Fund Manager North – husband Ifan

Simon Bell – Maxim's Solicitor – wife Zita

Megan Carr – Briefly Fund Manager North

Theo Clark – Minister of Public Affairs

Mary Davey – employee – North – sacked when at husband's bedside

Linda Downey – sacked employee north

Petra Evansen – Gina's friend – husband Bob

Gina Fiddes – main character – husband Greg daughter Gillian

Troy Finn – Minister of Health

Jane and Nico Gerrard – Maxim's house staff

Ben and John Haan – reporters

Don Hale – friend of Gina's

David Johannes – acquaintance

Rissa Lancie – Angelus Manager – aka Nerissa Vasca, Neri Samuel

Damon Long – Angelus Trustee

Ranek Malesh – Angelus Trustee aka Boran Myan

Anya Marley – Angelus employee – North

Trevor Mason – Chairman of EST (Emergency Services Trust)

Felix Mergen – Angelus Trustee

Konrad Nage – President of the Republic of Cymran – wife Janine

Fay and Lars Nielson – friends of Gina

Pascal and Pierre Niven – (twins) – Investigators

Seth Novak – Senior, Special Security Officer

Sonja Peters – Special Security Officer

Tony Rohm – First General Manager of Angelus Charity

Grace and James Samuel – adopted Rissa when four

Marcus Temple – Chairman of the Angelus Charity Board of Trustees

Colin Toben – Angelus Trustee

Myra Vasca – Rissa's natural mother

Viana Weiss – employee South

Carl Wykes – Paramedic Manager

Maxim Xavier – generous benefactor of the Angelus